An Intertwined Reality

Short Stories for the Already but Not Yet

by Eric Verbovszky

Copyright © 2013 by Eric Verbovszky

www.thekayakingchurch.com

ISBN: 1489541306
ISBN-13: 978-1489541307

All Rights Reserved.

Acknowledgements

Thank you to everyone, family and friends, who gave me encouragement, instruction, and feedback. Thank you to everyone who went to my website and actually read my stories when I sent you an email!

Thank you to the Church for being the agent of God's love and redemption to a broken and hurting world. I pray that the Church will continue to explore and focus on our mission of holy love in this time of the Already but Not Yet.

*These stories are dedicated to anyone searching for hope;
true hope is only found in the love of God, made known
through the Father, the Son, and the Holy Spirit.*

Contents:

Introduction   1

Babble, Part One   3
Seven Days   17
The Defeat of the Amorites   21
After Death   29
Antietam   47
1 Kings 12   53
The Fall of Belshazzar   59
The Ammonite Messenger   65
Luke 9:23   69
Babble, Part Two   73
Across an Ocean   77
Of Pigeons and Oilmen   95
A Tale of Wisdom and Folly   101
Babble, Part Three   105

Appendices   121

Scripture References   123
Reflections on the Writing Process   125
On Love   131

Introduction

Matthew 6:10

Your kingdom come. Your will be done, on earth as it is in heaven.

—

In the midst of preaching his "Sermon on the Mount," Jesus Christ uttered these words to the crowd gathered around him. God incarnate - the Son of God and the Son of Man - challenged his disciples about what it truly meant to follow God. Almost two millennia later, the truth of Christ's message in Matthew 5 to 7 still applies to us today.

These are chapters which challenge us to live in a way that is representative of the kingdom of God; we follow Christ's example while living in a world once perfected in love, but now broken in sin and selfishness. It is by no means easy; in fact, to truly follow Christ is perhaps one of the most difficult ways to live. And while God, in his inherent mysteriousness and holiness, does not always give us the answers, he does give us both love and faith, critical characteristics of anyone claiming to represent the kingdom of God. By these traits we pray, act, and live in the way that Christ instructed in Matthew 6:9-13, "The Lord's Prayer": "Your kingdom come. Your will be done, on earth as it is in heaven."

We live in the intersection of two worlds. This intersection is an age where death and its consequences run rampant, yet it is also an age where the reality of God's life-giving and eternal kingdom is breaking into our present era. At the center of this intersection is Christ's life, death, and resurrection. It is the 'Already' - the work of God's redeeming love in this fallen age, molding and shaping it into the 'Not Yet' - a new creation, resurrected and free from the bondage of death.

May the stories I have included in this anthology challenge you to consider what it means to live in the "Already but Not Yet," this intertwined reality of two eras.

May these stories challenge you to think more deeply about what it means to be a representative of God's kingdom here on earth.

May these stories challenge you to reflect on God himself and learn about God's mysteriousness and holiness in faithfulness and love.

And may these stories challenge you to not only consider God's kingdom coming into a world broken by sin so long ago, but also to look to the hope of a restored earth, perfected in love by God, in the certainty of a new era to come.

These 14 short stories are a reflection of what the world once was, what it currently is, and what it is yet to become. This is the intertwined reality that we live in.

I sincerely hope you enjoy them.

Babble, Part One

"I never quite under-ssss-stood why everyone calls him 'The High Dweller,'" Mrs. Nachosh stated. She spoke slowly and had the habit of hissing whenever she made an 's' sound.

I looked down below me as I listened to Mrs. Nachosh. A small brown mouse was taking a walk on the lush lawn. The animal, which appeared to be hunting for seeds, was dwarfed by the large green blades of grass. A cat with spotted fur followed the mouse quietly; except for the mouse lifting its head up every once in a while, sniffing the air around him, he didn't seem to notice the bigger creature behind him. Mrs. Nachosh saw me glance down at the ground.

"Is everything okay?" she asked. "Oph?" I turned my head back to Mrs. Nachosh. "You seem quite distracted today."

"Ah, I'm doing fine," I replied.

Mrs. Nachosh resumed her conversation. "I just never understood why. It seems like 'The High Dweller' is only half the description. He's always taking walks in the garden. He's always talking to us. The name 'The High Dweller' just implies that he only lives sssssss-somewhere else." She gave an especially long hiss as she said the word 'somewhere.' She looked up through the tree top towards the rich blue sky. "Like he *only* lives up there."

I nodded my head, trying to pay attention to her.

"A more accurate name might be 'The In Dweller.' He doesn't dwell simply above us. He dwells with us! His sssssss-spirit even dwells inside of us." She paused once more. "It is only his spirit that gives us life." She stopped mid-thought and turned her head towards the ground as well. "Look! Tsiyyi is out again. I wonder if Akbar is there with him too; I can't see so well today. My eyes are cloudy. They have always been such great friends since they were so young. I believe they are about the same age as you, Oph?"

"They are, Mrs. Nachosh."

"There is such beauty and harmony in this garden." She looked around at the various trees surrounding the open patch of grass beneath us. She must have been cultivating another line of thought as she continued to observe the garden in silence.

"I've always wondered how long we've been here. It seems like forever. They say that 'The High Dweller' just told the land and the seas to produce life. And they did! Quite amazing, if I must ssssss-say sss-so my-sssss-self. But I don't think anyone quite knows how long it's-sss actually been. I sss-suppose I could ask my parents or my parents' parents-ss. Or maybe even my parents' parents' parents-ss. They've been alive quite a long time! My parents-sss' parents-sss' parents-sss' parents-sss may even ssss-still be around somewhere. Although I heard they took a vacation a few years ago. Not sure if they came back yet or not. There are so many lovely places around here. I wouldn't be surprised if they ss-suddenly found a new beautiful place to ss-settle down and sssss-stay there."

I knew what I was getting myself into when I decided to visit Mrs. Nachosh; she always liked to engage in deeper conversations as she reflected on her life. But even I was having a hard time keeping track of the generations of her parents' parents' parents' parents, or however many parents' parents were in her family. Mr. and Mrs. Nachosh were already fairly old with children, grandchildren, and great-grandchildren. I'd be lost if I tried to grasp how many Nachosh generations were actually alive.

Mr. and Mrs. Nachosh were wise and gave good advice, although only Mrs. Nachosh was around today. I suppose I stopped in to see them for that reason, even if I didn't realize it at first.

The truth was that I really was distracted. Something within me was changing. It felt as if my whole physical being was on its way toward a state of flux; it grew from deep within my heart. I had always been very happy; I had been born a long time even after Mr. and Mrs. Nachosh married one another. But for as long as I had been alive, everyone I knew had been remarkably joyful. They passed that joy along to me. With my parents, my grandparents, my great-grandparents, my great-great-grandparents, and all my other relatives, I have only known joy, contentment, peace, and fulfillment. This feeling, though, was something more; it was as if this happiness, joy, contentment, peace, and fulfillment had been energized.

This sudden feeling only happened when I thought of her. Whenever I would think of her, see her, or spend any time with her, even if it was just for a minute or two, my heart began to beat two or three times faster, filing my entire body with this overwhelming joy. The peace and contentment that I had known my whole life suddenly manifested itself in a new level that I had never experienced before.

Mrs. Nachosh looked at me, stuck her tongue out quickly, and realized what was happening. "Oph! I should have known right away! You are in love. I can tell; I can see it within you. It is the sssss-same feeling I knew when Mr. Nachosh and I first began to ss-see one another so long ago. Everything you are feeling – it is called love. You've known love your whole life, given to you by your family, friends, and by 'The High – or rather – In – Dweller' him-ss-self, but now it has grown into a greater love!" I smiled as Mrs. Nachosh spoke. "What is her name?" the old serpent asked.

"Her name is Yaphah. We grew up together. Her family moved near mine when I was young. She is beautiful. Her eyes are breathtaking. She has the most stunning red feathers on her tail. She is the most amazing bird I have ever seen."

"Does she know how you feel?" Mrs. Nachosh asked.

"I don't think so."

"You should bring her a gift!"

"You think so?" Mrs. Nachosh smiled, affirming her thoughts. "She likes twigs and plants for her home. Maybe I will gather some and bring them to her. I bet she would love some leafy twigs."

"Don't forget flowers."

"I will get a flower for her too."

"Oph, you and Yaphah will make a truly lovely pair of hawks-sss." Mrs. Nachosh continued to smile as she said those words. "This brings back ss-so many memories of Mr. Nachosh and me when we were young." She stopped speaking as she looked around once more, unwinding her body through the higher branches of the tree, pushing here and there with one of her four short legs in order to get a better view of the garden. "Speaking of Mr. Nachosh, he has just not been him-sss-self recently. I don't know what has gotten in to him. He is usually ssss-so happy! But he's just been traip-sssse-ing around the last couple days. His eyes are always downcast. I don't know what to think! I've never ss-seen anything like it before! Ever – and I'm old. Ssssss-sometimes he just ss-slithers on his belly, without even using his legs, like he's lost his pride." She paused and stuck her tongue out. "I'm sure he will be okay though. If I sss-see 'The High Dweller' walking in the garden today, I will ss-suggest it to him. He will know what to do. He always does. Or if I sss-see the humans, they may know what to do. 'The High Dweller' made them to be fairly sss-smart and wise creatures, if I can ssssss-say sss-so my-sssss-self."

"Thank you, Mrs. Nachosh, for your advice. I am going to find the perfect gift now." I extended my wings, giving a quick flap and gathering some initial lift to get myself afloat and off the tree branch. "If I see Mr. Nachosh, I will tell him that you are looking for him."

"Thank you, Oph. 'The High Dweller' certainly ble-sssss-ssed you with much better eye-sss-sight than he gave me."

I pushed off, gave my wings several more strong flaps, gaining elevation. Although we were already in the tree's highest branches, I decided that I would swoop down to the lawn below and say hello to my friends Akbar the mouse and Tsiyyi the cat. Letting the air fly through my feathers as I soared down, I quickly scanned the area for Mr. Nachosh. I couldn't see him anywhere. He and Mrs. Nachosh always seemed to be inseparable, the two old green scaly serpents coiled up next to one another in the same leafy tree.

Approaching the ground, I flapped my wings a few times to slow my descent, and landed next to the mouse and the cat.

"Hey Oph!" Akbar spoke.

Tsiyyi looked over. "Great to see you, Oph! You always dive in so fast; I never know when you're coming!"

"I was just speaking to Mrs. Nachosh in the tree and saw you both down here. So I decided to say hello. Anyway, I've gotta fly! I'm going to go find Yaphah."

Tsiyyi and Akbar looked at each other. "So you're finally going to go talk to her?" Tsiyyi said.

"Yeah! I'm going to give her some leafy twigs. She loves those kinds of things. And a flower too." I grinned. Tsiyyi looked like he was trying to hold back laughter. "Some day you will find some cat to fall in love with too. Then you'll be coming to me for help!" Tsiyyi peered behind me. I turned around. Another spotted cat was laying by a tree, taking a nap in the shade. "So you've already found her! You should do what Mrs. Nachosh suggested. Bring her a gift that she will like!"

Tsiyyi grinned as well. "Okay. Okay. That's a good idea."

Akbar spoke up. The mouse looked so small next to Tsiyyi and me. "How are Mr. and Mrs. Nachosh doing? They've always been so nice to me."

"Well, only Mrs. Nachosh was in their tree today. She said

Mr. Nachosh has been acting funny. If you see him around, tell him that Mrs. Nachosh is looking for him."

"He might be headed to the center of the garden. I saw him walking in that direction yesterday," Tsiyyi replied.

"They say Mrs. Nachosh might be hundreds of years old. I don't even know if the two humans are that old!" Akbar stated.

"I don't think they are. One time she told me that 'The High Dweller' personally made the two humans. He made one a man and the other a woman, almost making them like him." I looked around again at the garden. There were so many trees, plants, and flowers. "But he took his time with all of this, like an artist. Today she told me that once 'The High Dweller' finished making the land and the waters, he simply told them to produce life! And then creatures like you and me started to appear. But he made the humans last. Although it does seem like they've been around for a really long time. But I don't think anyone knows how long it's been since 'The High Dweller' started the whole process."

Akbar began speaking again. "Mr. Koach has been around for a while. He might know. I think that old turtle is an artist too." Akbar paused. "He might paint."

Tsiyyi and I looked at Akbar strangely. "Paint?"

Akbar looked back at both of us, casting his gaze at me, then at Tsiyyi, then back at me. "Yeah. He paints." Neither Tsiyyi nor I knew what 'paint' was. Besides the turtle, Mr. Koach, it was probably some activity that the humans also do. There was a slightly longer pause after Akbar made his remark. I took it as my opportunity to leave; I couldn't really contribute a lot to a conversation about whatever 'paint' was.

"Well, I've gotta fly and find some good leafy twigs before the sun sets. Friends, I will see you two later!"

I gave several strong flaps of my wings and began my flight, leaving the cat and mouse behind me. I already knew my plan: I would find several leafy twigs, put them in a bundle, and then bind the bundle together with a beautiful flower. I would make it to Yaphah's tree just in time for the sunset! Though it wouldn't take long to find the leafy twigs, it might take a little longer to find the perfect flower.

Gaining more elevation and climbing above the treetops, I finally caught a glimpse of Mr. Nachosh. Just as Tsiyyi had mentioned, he was by a tree in the center of the garden. The serpent was talking with the two humans. The woman, whom all the other creatures I knew called 'Life,' was holding a piece of the tree's fruit in her hand. In all my flights over the garden, I couldn't ever recall seeing the man and the woman by this tree; it was a bit puzzling for a few moments.

I couldn't explain why, but my heart stopped for a moment as I watched the scene beneath me. For just a second, I lost energy and couldn't catch my breath. It seemed like something was wrapping itself around my stomach and my throat, squeezing them. The odd sensation left in an instant; it was gone almost as soon as it came over me.

I never felt anything like it before. I could imagine that if there was an opposite experience to what my love for Yaphah felt like, this would have been it.

I looked back up towards the sky; the sun was going to set in another hour! I needed to gather the twigs and flower quickly, get them wrapped up, and then take them to Yaphah before dark. Telling Mr. Nachosh that Mrs. Nachosh was looking for him would have to wait until later. Besides, if I told him now, even if I did it fast, he might still draw me into a long conversation. Serpents are like that.

I spotted a thick forested area on the far side of the garden that I knew would guarantee plenty of leafy twigs. Gathering some speed, I dove and landed at the edge of the section of the woods.

The trees in this area were a lot taller than the ones in the grove where Mr. and Mrs. Nachosh, Akbar, and Tsiyyi lived; it must have been a much older part of the garden. The air grew cooler as I strolled under the canopy. It was shadowy and dark; not as much sun was able to sneak through the forest's tree tops to provide light and warmth. I felt the same sensation, but much more faintly, that I did when I flew over Mr. Nachosh, the man, and the woman by the tree in the center of the garden. If I found the twigs and flower quickly, I could get out of this forest and back into the sunlight; then hopefully this feeling would pass.

I spotted several nice sized leafy twigs laying on the ground next to me. I picked three of them up with my beak; they weren't too heavy and they weren't too light. They were just perfect! They even had the right amount of green leaves still attached to them. All I had left was to find the perfect flower to wrap up the twigs with! Jumping up on a small rock, I scanned a little deeper in the cold and shadowy forest.

I found it! I would have to fly further in the woods, but it was there. It was growing underneath a tall pine tree. I picked up the leafy twigs with my beak, pumped my wings, and flew through the undergrowth to the flower.

The flower was vibrant purple. Although its beauty competed with the beauty of Yaphah, it did not match it; nothing could match her beauty. I set the twigs down next to the flower and bit the base of the stem with my beak, breaking it off from the ground. Very carefully, I set it on the ground; I did not want to disturb any of the petals. I put the twigs on top of the stem and cautiously tied the stem around the small branches. Taking a step back, I looked at the finished creation; it was perfect for Yaphah! I had no doubt that she would enjoy this gift. I put my beak around the completed present and lifted it up.

The air was still becoming cooler and darker. A tingling sensation crept across the feathers on my back. Something strange was happening here; I needed to get out of the forest and back into the sunlight.

As I extended my wings, I saw something peculiar. A brown leaf floated down to the ground next to me; its edges were curled up. I had never seen anything like it before; all the leaves I had ever seen in my life were always a lush green. I glanced above me; the forest, for the most part, was green, but I saw more brown leaves mixed in the canopy leaves, several of them floating to the ground. The forest was changing right before my very eyes. Even when I flew in and landed at the edge of these woods, I did not see any brown leaves. My heart shuddered again with the same feeling

I had when I saw the serpent talking to the man and the woman by the tree in the center of the garden.

I took a breath, vigorously pumped my wings, and flew straight out of the forest. The sunlight immediately calmed me once I got to the open air. A surge of life ran through me once more as I breathed in the fresh air of the garden. Maybe what Mrs. Nachosh said about the spirit of 'The High Dweller' giving all creatures life was true. I took one more deep breath and looked toward the horizon; the base of the sun was already beginning to dip below the skyline. I had to get to Yaphah right away!

Flapping my wings, I climbed high above the treetops, turned in the direction of the tree grove where Yaphah and her family made their nest, spread my wings, and soared. Returning over the center of the garden, Mr. Nachosh and the two humans were gone.

I landed on the branch outside Yaphah's nest; their tree was not far from the grove where Mr. and Mrs. Nachosh, Akbar, and Tsiyyi lived. Yaphah's family made their nest pretty high in the tree; hawks usually like the height. I set my gift down gently on the branch, inspecting it one last time. Everything looked good. My heart was beating fast; I wasn't sure if it was because I had just flown over the garden so quickly, or because I was about to see this beautiful hawk and was nervous. I felt the joy, contentment, peace, and fulfillment within me growing into what Mrs. Nachosh called love, all directed toward Yaphah.

Another hawk landed on the branch. It was Yaphah's father. I had met him several times before.

"Can I help you, Oph?"

"Is...." I paused and took a deep breath. "Is Yaphah here?"

"She is. Let me get her. I'm sure she will be right down." Yaphah's father flew up to a higher branch.

I took another breath.

"Oph?" It was Yaphah. I looked at her. She was as beautiful as she had always been. Her eyes were piercing, yet calm and full of the love that she had known her whole life. Her feathers were shining as the sun cast a golden hue over them. Behind her were shades of purple, red, yellow, and orange as the sun dipped further below the horizon.

"Maybe this is what Akbar was referring to when he was talking about 'paint.'" I didn't really know what to say.

"What? Paint?" Yaphah responded.

"Yeah. Paint," I replied. I still didn't know exactly what I should say. I don't think I was making sense to Yaphah. "Hi." I started over. "I...I...got you something." I picked up the gift, hopped closer to her, and set it down on the branch before her. "I know how much you like twigs. I got them from the forest on the other side of the garden. I found this flower for you too. I thought you'd like it."

I looked at Yaphah, unsure of what she would say. My heart was still beating fast. Yaphah smiled.

"Oph, it's beautiful! Thank you so much!" Yaphah turned and looked at the sunset. "Do you want to fly together before it gets dark?" I smiled back at Yaphah. Mrs. Nachosh had the perfect advice; she truly was one wise old serpent. Although, all of the serpents I had ever run into in the garden had been both crafty and wise.

"A sunset flight sounds like a great idea."

As I extended my wings, the feeling that I had when I flew over the center of the garden, and when I was in the forest, abruptly returned. It was much stronger this time; there was nothing I could do to stop it. My stomach tightened. I started to get a headache. I had a hard time breathing. Yaphah became blurry even though she was right in front of me. I started to lose my balance on the tree branch and took a step back. Confusion was clouding my mind.

"Oph? Are you okay?" I heard Yaphah ask. She became more blurry.

"I...I... don't...think....." I lost my balance again. I took another step back, but there was no more branch to step on. I began to fall. I tried to pump my wings, but I had no energy and continued to drop. Everything was blurry and my head was really hurting.

"Oph! Oph!" As I fell, I saw another bird flap their wings and fly toward me. It could've been Yaphah. If it was Yaphah, she flew underneath me and caught me, saving my life before I crashed into the ground.

"Oph! What happened?"

"I...I...." I didn't know who or what Oph was.

As I lay on the ground, and even with my worsening vision, pounding headache, and confusion, I discerned a large spotted cat pounce on a mouse, then carry its limp body in its mouth. A serpent was crawling toward me, its tongue slipping in and out of its mouth. The cat and the mouse and the snake looked so familiar; the bird next to me seemed familiar. The serpent suddenly lifted up the upper half of its body, rearing its head back and opening its mouth, showing razor sharp teeth.

"Mr. Nachosh! What are you doing?" I heard the bird next to me speak.

"Ssss-silen-ssssss-ce! I am not Mr. Nachosh!" The serpent hissed before snapping its head in the direction of the other bird that was next to me.

Unable to move, my head rested in the grass. The purple flower and the twigs had been knocked off the branch; they were laying near me on the ground now. The petals of the once beautiful and rich purple flower were beginning to turn brown. Its edges were curling upwards.

I heard another voice; it was very faint, yet extremely familiar. I knew that this voice had a name, but I couldn't recall what it was called or where I had heard it before.

The voice was calling for the two humans to come to him.

Seven Days

Two small cardboard boxes sat on the carpeted floor of the family room; inside the boxes were a few random, last-minute items, including three frayed toothbrushes, a half-empty tube of toothpaste, a couple washrags, a fifty cent bar of soap, and a small stuffed whale that belonged to their young daughter. A lone light-blue laundry basket rested next to the two boxes; it was not overflowing with clothes. The folded shirts, pants, dresses, and jackets inside barely reached the top of the basket. The woman and the girl sat on the tan, sand-colored couch as the man sat on the wooden rocking chair, the husband and wife staring with doubtful eyes at the three containers between them. The father had no desire to rock back and forth on the chair as he leaned forward, his elbows resting on his legs, and his hands together with his fingers interlaced, manifesting the worry in his heart. In the days to come he knew he would need all the stability he could find.

His daughter gazed at her father; she did not know what was happening, but she knew something was not right as she sought the comfort which she learned she could always find in her father's loving eyes. The man warmly looked back at his daughter, trying to force a small smile despite the circumstances. A small stream of sunlight trickled its way through the curtains covering the window, finally falling on the small stuffed whale unsuccessfully swimming at the top of one of the cardboard boxes.

As they waited in silence, the man, his wife, and his daughter listened to the slow drip of water fall from the faucet every few minutes, hitting the barren sink underneath. In the seven years that they lived in their small but comfortable house, the man had never been able to fix the slow leak; it would have required getting a brand new faucet, but that would have cost money that his family could not spare. Making the choice between food and heat in the winter, or fixing a minor faucet problem presented no difficulty for him.

The woman turned her right wrist toward her, studying the time-piece on her lower arm. The watch had a worn, brown leather strap from the years of its use, but it never stopped working. As he continued staring at the three containers in the middle of the room, contemplating the inevitable moment that was to come, the woman's husband saw her check the watch from the corner of his eye.

He gave it to her on their first wedding anniversary. It was brand new back then; he saved his money for months to buy it for her after he first heard her mention that she would like one. He lifted his head and studied the beauty of his wife's face as she looked at her watch. The thought of not being able to provide the happiness that he wanted for the two loves of his life was held in check only by a faint grain of hope in his mind. He dwelled on the thought for perhaps a few too many seconds; but as he considered the woman sitting across from him, he realized that despite everything, she was still wearing that same watch, no matter how worn the brown leather band appeared to be.

The dreadful knock on the door did not echo through the empty house; the three short taps coming from the front of their home told the husband and wife that the man from the bank finally arrived. Holding her daughter's small hand, they stood up from the sand-colored couch. The girl's father rose to his feet from the wooden rocker, releasing the chair from its long-held tension. He took a step toward his wife, touched her right hand, and kissed her. He peered down at his daughter and put his hand on her head; she looked back up at him with a comforting smile.

The girl's mother reached down to pick up one of the small cardboard boxes. The girl followed her mother's example and picked up the box that held her stuffed whale. The father picked up the lone light-blue laundry basket with their clothes. All three walked toward the front door, heading toward their sedan parked in front of the house that would shortly no longer be their home. The sedan already had the remainder of their few possessions securely packed away. They sold their van months ago in an effort to ward off homelessness for a little while longer.

The father set down the basket as he opened the door, silently handing the man from the bank the keys to the house, staring at him with inhospitable eyes as his wife and daughter passed through the door. Both of them avoided eye contact with this stranger who had come to take their home away. The man from the bank turned his eyes to the ground in discomfort; he wanted to avoid the shame of casting yet another family into roofless uncertainty while, at the same time, knowing the number of empty houses that the bank owned. The banker heard a feeble drip come from the kitchen a few feet away.

The mother, father, and daughter walked down the short

concrete path leading to their sedan, passing by the flower bed of white impatiens glowing in the afternoon sun. None of them looked back to the foreclosed house behind them.

They squeezed the three containers into the backseat before the mother and father safely strapped the seatbelt over their daughter, the final dismal click resonating in the parents' ears. They looked at their daughter in that moment with as much hope as they could find within their hearts before getting into the car themselves. The man turned the car on; the gas gauge moved upwards with the dull hum of the engine. There was enough gas to get to his wife's sisters' home a few hours away in the next state. Taking one more look out the driver side window before shifting the car in reverse, he saw a dove land on the concrete path they just walked down; a small branch was in its mouth. A green leaf still clung to the tiny twig that the white bird carried.

He looked over toward his wife, the small seed of hope within him giving his eyes the determined strength that his family needed to see. As he turned to look in the rear-view mirror, he watched his daughter play with the stuffed whale, finally swimming free from the constraints of the small box. The man placed his hand on the gear shifter. He felt his wife place her hand on top of his in the moment before they left; when he looked down he saw the worn, brown leather band and the never-failing watch on her wrist.

His heart rested; there was no need to worry. He did not know how long they would be at sea, but he had faith that solid ground would be beneath his family's feet once again.

The Defeat of the Amorites

Adoni-zedek wanted to look into his captor's eyes one last time before his inevitable death; Joshua, the leader of this rogue band of invaders, had his foot firmly placed on the humiliated king's exposed neck. As the man labored to breathe under the weight of the Israelite, Adoni-zedek attempted to turn his head from the dust and back toward Joshua. It was one last effort to regain some show of honor. It was not for anyone else; it was for himself.

Days earlier, the five deposed kings fled in cowardice as their soldiers died mercilessly at the hands of the foreigners. Joshua's loyal fighters now pressed their feet into the other leaders' necks, the toppled kings grasping to hold onto their last moments of life before the Hebrew swords put a final end to their existence. Dragged out from the cave in Makkedah, the Amorite kings hid in disgrace and shame while their armies were hunted down.

Adoni-zedek squinted as he and the other kings were pulled into the daylight and thrown onto the rocky ground outside, the bright sun shocking their dim eyes which had become so accustomed to the darkness. He did not understand any of the words the foreign soldiers were saying to one another; even before one of the men, who gave commands and appeared to be the leader of the group, moved toward Adoni-zedek, the king of Jerusalem recognized the futility of escape. He knew that this would be the end.

—

"King," the courier stated after bowing before Adoni-zedek. The court's messenger looked reluctantly at the king of Jerusalem. He was afraid to give the king news that he knew Adoni-zedek would not want to hear. The courier took a breath before attempting to speak. He looked back down at the ground. His lips trembled as he started to give his report. "The spies...the spies...they've reported...they've...." The courier stammered.

Adoni-zedek was already anticipating bad news. He rose from his throne. "Look at me and speak!" he commanded. The king's voice boomed in the nearly empty room.

The messenger looked up once more, doing his best to show confidence to the king. Adoni-zedek stared intently at the courier as he waited for the information. "The spies...they've reported...Gibeon has made peace with the Israelites. And...the Gibeonites will join them in battle." The courier took a deep breath. Although he was relieved to finally provide the intelligence to Adoni-zedek, he was unsure of how the king would react. The courier waited for the king's answer.

Adoni-zedek sat back down in his throne. He was not angry, at least not yet. As far as the messenger could tell, the king showed a rare moment of despair. "You're sure?" Adoni-zedek asked after a brief pause.

"Yes," the courier replied, still expecting the king of Jerusalem's response to shift to his usual vexed disposition.

The king leaned forward as he thought of his options. The messenger waited nervously. Several minutes later, he finally spoke. "Send in my scribe." The king looked at the courier and raised his voice. "Immediately!" The courier hurried out of the king's throne room, thankful to dodge the worst of Adoni-zedek's wrath.

The king of Jerusalem knew that these foreign invaders were coming. Alarming reports came in the previous weeks and months from both his allies and his various rural outposts. These were a group of people who completely destroyed Ai. And if the rumors were true, the Israelites completely razed Jericho to the ground simply by marching around the walled city.

Adoni-zedek's scribe appeared in the room, bowing before the king.

"Come!" Adoni-zedek beckoned him. "And write everything I say!"

The scribe shuffled forward; like the courier, he also did not know what to expect from the king. As the scribe glanced at Adoni-zedek, he noticed the king's impatient look.

"Quickly!" The king ordered. "There is not a lot of time. Put the ink to paper and start writing!" The scribe rushed to a chair by the king of Jerusalem. His hands fumbled for a moment as he searched for the quill, ink, and parchment in his small bag. The scribe knew that Adoni-zedek was not known for his restraint. After a few more tense seconds, he was ready to write the king's words. Adoni-zedek began to speak:

> "To the Amorite Kings; to King Hoham of Hebron; to King Piram of Jarmuth; to King Japhia of Lachish; and to King

Debir of Eglon:

"Jericho's walls have fallen in only a week; their king is dead, murdered by a band of foreign invaders from the west. Ai has fallen; their king, too, is dead, slaughtered by the approaching enemy. They are led by a man known as Joshua, a powerful warrior who has united these vagrants. I do not know by what unseen force they fight with, whether it is some new magic, or some unknown Hebrew god who has blessed them, but it is some strength that will be beyond our individual power if we choose to stand against these Israelites alone. If we do not unite our armies and fight, our kingdoms will fall. Our reigns as kings will end. They will show no mercy. I do not write these words lightly, and I know you may find them difficult to read, for I know of your pride in your military might. But our pride does not always reflect our reality.

"I know each of you have heard reports from your spies and messengers; you fear not simply this band of attacking vagrants, but the unknown power that is with them. Our only chance to repel the enemy at our gates is to unite and demonstrate the full capabilities of our combined armies.

"I have reliable intelligence that the Gibeonites have made peace with the Israelites. In order to gain victory, we must set up an ambush at Gibeon. We will destroy the traitors. And we will destroy Joshua and the Israelites. I ask that you assemble your soldiers and lead them to Gibeon. We will meet there in one week's time, we will attack, and we will preserve our Amorite kingdoms."

The king paused. The scribe waited for the king to dictate the next words. He looked up at Adoni-zedek; the king of Jerusalem gazed ahead, pondering what else he could say. Finally, he spoke again. "Sign the letter in my name. Write a copy for each of the Amorite kings, close them with my seal, and have the fastest couriers dispatched with the letters to these lands immediately."

The scribe nodded.

"Now get out," the king commanded. The scribe gathered his quill, ink, and parchment and hurried out of Adoni-zedek's throne room.

—

Joshua's sharpened blade, shining in the hot desert sun, clean from the stains of Amorite blood, came crashing down, beheading the once great king. Adoni-zedek's head rolled back to the side; the king of Jerusalem's eyes once again returned to stare at the dust. The swords of Joshua's soldiers followed, slicing through the air, decapitating Hoham of Hebron, Piram of Jarmuth, Japhia of Lachish, and Debir of Eglon.

—

An Intertwined Reality: Short Stories for the Already but Not Yet

Joshua 10: 6 – 15

And the Gibeonites sent to Joshua at the camp in Gilgal, saying, "Do not abandon your servants; come up to us quickly, and save us, and help us; for all the kings of the Amorites who live in the hill country are gathered against us." So Joshua went up from Gilgal, he and all the fighting force with him, all the mighty warriors. The LORD said to Joshua, "Do not fear them, for I have handed them over to you; not one of them shall stand before you." So Joshua came upon them suddenly, having marched up all night from Gilgal. And the LORD threw them into a panic before Israel, who inflicted a great slaughter on them at Gibeon, chased them by the way of the ascent of Beth-horon, and struck them down as far as Azekah and Makkedah. As they fled before Israel, while they were going down the slope of Beth-horon, the LORD threw down huge stones from heaven on them as far as Azekah, and they died; there were more who died because of the hailstones than the Israelites killed with the sword.

On the day when the LORD gave the Amorites over to the Israelites, Joshua spoke to the LORD; and he said in the sight of Israel, "Sun, stand still at Gibeon, and Moon, in the valley of Aijalon."

And the sun stood still, and the moon stopped, until the nation took vengeance on their enemies.

Is this not written in the Book of Jashar? The sun stopped in midheaven, and did not hurry to set for about a whole day. There has been no day like it before or since, when the LORD heeded a human voice; for the LORD fought for Israel.

Then Joshua returned, and all Israel with him, to the camp at Gilgal.

After Death

For the dead; may they rest in peace.

—

1 Samuel 28:14-16

He said to her, "What is his appearance?" She said, "An old man is coming up; he is wrapped in a robe." So Saul knew that it was Samuel, and he bowed with his face to the ground, and did obeisance.

Then Samuel said to Saul, "Why have you disturbed me by bringing me up?" Saul answered, "I am in great distress, for the Philistines are warring against me, and God has turned away from me and answers me no more, either by prophets or by dreams; so I have summoned you to tell me what I should do."

Samuel said, "Why then do you ask me, since the LORD has turned from you and become your enemy?"

—

It was not too long ago that there was a man who, after losing his job because of the economic downturn and the desire of the large business he worked for to put the acquisition of money over the welfare of people, died. He had two beautiful daughters and a beautiful wife and did his best to take care of them despite his financial situation. However, one rainy evening, as he was returning from yet another interview for a job that did not care about his high level of education and the expertise he had in his field, and when the signal showed the little lit-up man which told pedestrians that it was okay to walk, he stepped off the curb of the sidewalk and was hit by a drunk driver who had also lost his job for the same reasons, but who dealt with it by daily drinking bottles of alcohol in an effort to bury his pain. The man was immediately killed.

During his life on earth, the man did not think much about what would happen after death.

But after he died, the man's soul plunged into the shadowy depths of what some call Sheol and what others call Hades.

And this is where the man's story begins – after death.

–

"Hey! What's your name?" I opened my eyes. I didn't know if I had been asleep, or how long I had been asleep, if that was the state which a person wanted to call it. I felt drowsy. I was light-headed. I didn't feel entirely there. But looking around, there was only darkness surrounding me. I at first didn't even know if my eyes were open or closed. It took a while for my eyes to adjust to the darkness. Again, I heard the strange voice call out, the sound being carried through the air, but not like any other sound I had heard in my life. Somehow I think the atmosphere of the place I was in was affecting the way I heard the person's voice. If an adjective could be put to the person's voice, it was that the voice was airy, just like I felt airy. Everything was airy in this place. And although it was airy, it also felt damp. It was as if I was in a cave or some place like one.

Yet the dampness made the air feel heavy. It was an odd mixture of being heavily airy. It probably contributed to my light-headedness.

The airy voice called to me again. "Hey! What's your name?" My eyes started to adjust to the darkness, and for a moment I thought I saw a wisp of a shadow of some type of object in the corner of my eye. I couldn't look directly at it at first, for it kept moving as if it was floating. But, for sure, there was some kind of wispy shadow there, and it sounded like the voice was coming from it. If I didn't know any better, I would've thought it was a ghost.

Finally I forced the heavy air out of my mouth in response. "Hello?" I questioned, not sure to whom, or what, I was talking.

"Hey!" The voice responded.

"Where am I? I was just about to cross the street," I paused for a moment. "And I woke up here. Is this a hospital?" I stopped, pondering my question, and realized the answer to my own question. This place was by no means any type of hospital.

"Ha ha ha!" The shadowy, ghost-like wisp let out an airy, oddly pitched, laugh. I still couldn't see the figure entirely. "I suppose it could be called a hospital of sorts. A hospital for the dead!"

I thought to myself in shock. *The dead? A hospital for the dead?* I looked down at my arms. They were only shadows – faint outlines of what used to be a physical reality. Smoky, foggy, wisps of arms – and for that matter, the rest of my body too – just like the ghost I had been talking to.

"You know you're dead, right?" The ghost had somehow gauged that I hadn't even realized my own condition. "You passed over the river Styx, well, some time ago. Don't know exactly when, though. There's not really any idea of time down here. We're all just kind of ... floating around. Ha!" The ghost let out another airy laugh at his own joke.

I thought for sure that the river Styx was only Greek mythology. Evidently, though, the Greeks were on to something.

"You had coins in your eyes and everything!" The ghost laughed at me again.

"Do not listen to him," another voice spoke, coming from another shadowy wisp somewhere in this cave, or realm, that I ended up in. "There were no coins in your eyes. But you are dead. You are in what the Greeks called Hades and what the Hebrews called Sheol."

I looked around to see where the voice was coming from. As I turned around, or, I suppose, floated around would be the more proper way to say it, a figure appeared before me. He was clearly human, yet not physical, but had an appearance of a Native American. He seemed to be sitting down, poking what looked to be a fire which was not actually a fire, and smoking a pipe which was not actually a pipe, yet there was still smoke coming from the end of it. I maneuvered myself toward him.

"Join me," the figure spoke again. From what I could tell, the ghost, who was still chuckling at my expense, had drawn near to the Native American also.

"This is the ghost of a pirate, and even though we are all ghosts, he likes to call himself the ghost," the Native American said. He was silent after he spoke. He did not seem to be in a hurry to have a conversation. His patience made sense though. There was no reason to rush anything down here in the shadows of Sheol. I had no idea how much time had passed between the time he spoke and my response to him.

"What is this place?" I asked the Native American. He seemed to know more than the pirate's ghost.

The Native American's smoky eyes looked in my direction. "I told you. You are in the realm of the dead. It is what some here call Sheol and others here call Hades." The pirate's ghost laughed again. The Native American looked toward him.

"Nobody ever seems to want to realize that they're dead!" The ghost laughed.

The Native American expressed himself again. "The ghost is not always right, but he has spoken the truth this time. I passed into the sleep of death in what the Europeans called the year 1763. I was a great warrior and killed many in battle before encountering death myself. But I do not know how long ago that happened. It could have been days or years. Time no longer exists when one has crossed over the river Styx."

I asked myself if I even knew how long it had been since I died. I tried to think but I simply didn't know. I only became confused as the physical brain that I once had did not exist any more, no longer able to process the complexities of time's existence. For all I knew, it could have already been centuries or have only been minutes since I died. It could have been what they call in the physical life years that passed by between each sentence of the conversation that the Native American, the pirate's ghost, and I were having. After my spirit's mind tried to get the wispy remnants of any brain to consider the passing of time, I just couldn't comprehend it.

The Native American was right. There was no point in trying to contemplate time here. Life was over and there was no hurry now. And even though there was no time in shadowy Sheol, we had all the time in the world.

"What about you?" I asked the pirate's ghost. "What happened to you?"

"They hung me in 1707. I remember it clearly – a humid, sunny, summer day in the Caribbean. The British bastards sent me to the gallows and dropped the plank beneath me. My body plunged with the crunch of my neck and my soul fell into the realm of the Greeks. Believe it or not, I ran into a few of the Greeks some time ago. One of the guys claimed he was Achilles and said he actually died at Troy. I didn't believe it and started laughing at him!

"I suppose I deserved the death I received though. Who knows how many innocent souls I sent to Sheol during my own life, with burning towns and ships, looting, stealing, and everything else that went along with those sinful deeds. Most of them deserved what they got. Ha! I lived quite a horrible life. The bloody British were really right to hang me. Come to think of it, I don't blame them. I think they tossed my body in the ocean to be devoured by the sharks. No respect for the dead!" He stopped and started his odd laughing again. "Oh, I quite literally haunted the life out of those British swine who hung me. But I have always had plenty of fun!"

I don't think the pirate's ghost noticed my attempt to furrow my brow in confusion. I'm not sure how the Native American got so good at manipulating the appearance of his own spectral soul. The pirate's ghost, on the other hand, had no resemblance of a human. He was shapeless and shifty, just like the pirate he probably was in life. Faint wisps of the pirate's ghost appeared here and there.

The Native American noticed my confusion, although I don't know how. "The pirate's ghost leaves this realm all the time, returning to the physical world too many times. It is why he has no shape down here. He does not stay long enough for his soul to settle."

"How does he leave here?" I asked the Native American. The pirate's ghost laughed again.

"Sheol is not closed off for the dead. It is only closed off from the living. If the dead soul chooses, their soul may wander in and out of this realm and back into the earthly realm. But only here, in Sheol, will it rest in peace if the soul chooses to stay. At least it will find peace, if the rumors are true, until the day of resurrection."

The pirate's ghost muttered before I had a chance to ask more questions of the Native American. "Ha! You say peace. I say boredom! What fun is it to be content in death?" The pirate's gloomy ghost floated his shapeless cloud closer toward me. "You should see the amusement I have with some of the living! One day, I don't know when, but one day I was terrorizing this young child! I think she almost peed her pants! Ha ha ha! You should have seen the fear on her face! Give it a try sometime. Anyone you didn't like in your life? You could haunt and taunt them. Or I could give them a good scare for you!"

Immediately the thought of my old company, and my old boss there who fired me and was a real jerk, flashed through my mind. The thoughts of all those companies where I applied for work, and the people from those companies who interviewed me and didn't care, began passing through my mind too.

"You are becoming restless," the Native American spoke.

"What do you mean?" I asked him.

"Your form – if you do not find peace here, your form will become shapeless and void, like the pirate's ghost. Here, in Hades, is your opportunity to finally rest in peace. When you are at rest, your soul will find shape." Suddenly I understood, even though "suddenly" could have potentially been "slowly" over a really long period of time. Thinking in terms of time is a hard temptation to fight. The Native American, even though a ghost, had a clear shape. The pirate's ghost, on the other hand, did not. The Native American spoke again. "The more a soul wanders in and out of the depths of Sheol, the more their soul will become restless and the less likely it is that the soul will find peace."

"But the pirate's ghost – it seems to be having fun," I responded.

"So it appears. The pirate's ghost is only trying to convince himself that he is having fun. What fun could it be to terrorize young children as they seek peace and love in their own lives? The pirate's ghost does not know, or perhaps the pirate's ghost does know yet does not want to recognize it, that he will not find peace until he becomes content in his death. We have already lived our lives. We cannot bother those who are living theirs. We have already passed into this realm. There is nothing more we can offer the living except what we have already accomplished in life."

Silence followed. Again, I had no idea how long it was until he spoke once more. It could have very well been seconds, days, years, or even centuries or millennia before he talked again, but I had no way of knowing. As we waited in this vacuum of silence, I realized the truth he was speaking. It certainly made me aware of how much I wanted to do in life but did not get a chance to do, and how much more love I could have shown to my wife, children, and other friends during the time I had been allotted to walk the physical earth.

Sitting in silence with the Native American, I realized what the point of life was. It was not to participate in vanities, meaningless activities, and the relentless and worthless pursuit of money, fame, and power. But, at its simplest, most profound, and most focused, the point of life was simply to love one another. Money did not make the difference in the lives of the people I knew; only love made a difference for them. The more I pondered, the more I discerned that it was really only truly love that could overcome the violent evils of the physical realm. Even in my spectral state, I shuddered to think how often I had ignored that truth, and how often the people who were still blessed with life did not want to see the truth of love. Even the pirate's ghost in death could not realize it as he scared young children in his journeys in and out of Sheol. If people could just humble themselves to the point where they could show love to even their enemies, the vanities of violence would cease and the harmony of love would follow. In life there is the blessing of love, and only in love can the blessing of the physical realm be sincerely understood – I greatly desired that I had seen this basic truth before I passed over the river Styx.

The Native American looked over to me once more. "You have found peace. You are content. You are at rest." I looked at myself. Shadowy, cloud-like wisps defined my arms and legs much more clearly, even though I was still only a ghost, a soul, and a spirit, lacking any physical substance.

The Native American continued. "I do not know why I engaged in so much battle. I consider my life and realize that there was no point to the violence. There was only purpose in the harmony of loving one another. Love is true purpose. I only engaged in pointlessness; the Europeans engaged in pointlessness; all people in the physical realm probably continue to engage in pointlessness. There is nothing we can do now but pray for the living that they will see the truth of love. But even in life, selfishness and the evil it causes are unfortunately too unnaturally natural. It can only be overcome with the selflessness that seems so rare. But I am afraid that the living and the dead may not see a world of selflessness until the day of resurrection and the day of judgment."

"What do you mean by the day of resurrection?" I asked the Native American.

The pirate's ghost howled before the Native American could respond. "Damn priest!" I looked over to his shadowy form, hovering above the Native American's smoky fire which was not a real fire.

"I warned you," said the Native American. "When you wander the earth with your ghost, terrorizing the physical bodies of the living, one day you will encounter one who knows how to command you to find peace. And there will be nothing you can do except to listen. That person will command you to find peace not on their own authority, but on the authority of the one who created even this shadowy realm, allowing you and me the blessing of crossing the river Styx in peace."

"Damn it!" The pirate's ghost cursed again. "I was trying to have some fun. The child's family came in the room and then a priest came in. The family left and the priest stayed, and I knew that my time in the earthly realm was limited. The priest spoke some words in French and instructed me, in the name of you know – the one who will be at the day of resurrection and the day of judgment – to not leave the room. And I couldn't leave! I tried to escape his presence but I was bound by the authority of the one who will be at the day of resurrection and the day of judgment. Damn priest!"

I peered toward the shapeless form of the pirate's ghost. The Native American continued to look at his fire and smoke his pipe. "What happened next?" I asked the pirate's ghost.

"The priest commanded me to find peace in the sleep of death and then prohibited me from walking the earth, under the threat of a penalty of sure damnation at the day of resurrection and the day of judgment." The pirate's ghost, his foggy, cloud-like substance, hovered around the Native American and me once more. "Now I'm stuck here with the likes of you two boring people."

The Native American spoke. "I suggest you rest. You have not allowed yourself the freedom to rest in peace, despite whatever freedom you thought you had to roam the physical realm." The ghost quickly became a white cloud of smoke and then disappeared from view, probably off to another cavern of Hades to pout in frustration over what the French priest commanded him to do.

Silence followed once again. Minutes, days, years, centuries, or millennia may have passed without me knowing how long I had been asleep in death.

"What do both of you mean by the day of resurrection and the day of judgment?" I asked the Native American a second time.

"You have not heard the stories?" The Native American questioned me. "I thought for sure that you, a European, would have heard and heeded the stories. But I suppose no one anymore, and not even the souls down here, want to believe the stories anymore. I had heard parts of the stories in life but thought it was only another way the Europeans were trying to erase my people from the planet. So I ignored them and pursued a life of war. Although now that I have heard the truth of the stories, and have recognized the European's manipulations of the stories for what they were, I realize what many of those people were trying to say and live."

"What stories are you talking about?" I asked.

"There is a rumor between the ones who are in rest, and even among some who are still searching for rest, whether they know they are searching for rest or not, such as the pirate's ghost, that some time ago there was one who visited the depths of Sheol who had the authority to always cross over the river Styx freely in peace. This one had told the prophecy that he would one day bring a day of resurrection when our souls and spirits would be reunited with our bodies, and that judgment would be passed upon us after the examination of the condition of our hearts.

"If our hearts were found to be in selfless love, there would be life. If selfishness was discovered in our hearts, there would be no life and only eternal damnation." The Native American paused. "This is the damnation that the pirate's ghost spoke of when the priest warned him. Even the pirate's ghost fears it. That is why I encourage him to fnd peace. Only in peace can there be selflessness. Yet the prophecy continued by saying that only in the King could our souls truly find this life of selflessness and peace. I was not here when he came and I do not know when he came, but the ones who heard call him the King, for he had a crown upon his head.

"As I consider what my life was like, I wish that the Europeans did not manipulate his message. I realize now that even the revelation of peace and selflessness in life was given to my people before the Europeans came, yet many of my people, including myself, ignored it. I realize that this King is the incarnation of the revelation of peace and selflessness that so many around the world had known before many of the Europeans destroyed the message in greed. Now I choose to believe this prophecy. The King is just yet merciful, and I constantly pray that the King will not hold against me what I have done in life. May the King have mercy upon us all. However, if the King so chooses, he may even cast you and me into damnation for not responding in life and it will be in accordance with his justice. I do not know what will happen to our souls at the day of resurrection and the day of judgment upon the examination of our hearts, but I pray that the King may have mercy upon us all as we seek peace in our sleep of death."

"Do you really think the prophecy is true?" I asked the Native American.

"I must believe it. It is the only hope we have to experience the true beauty of love in the physical life once again. It is only in the physical unification of body and spirit with a heart that is restored in love that the goodness of the earth can be experienced. And only in the King can the heart be remade into a selfless love for people and other creatures. The stories end by saying that if selflessness is found in the individual's heart, that person will be allowed to live in the newly created physical creation which will exist in the harmony of love, fulfilling the prophecy of the King.

"I realize the error of the life I had in selfishness. May the King have mercy on me. May the King have mercy upon the living who do not realize the errors of their lives. May the King have mercy upon those who take for granted the blessing of a physical life in love."

The Native American and I sat in silence as the smoke floated out of his pipe with each of his breaths. Somewhere I heard the groans of the pirate's ghost as he wrestled with his own attempt to find peace.

"May the King even have mercy upon the pirate's ghost," the

Native American added. I prayed that the King would have mercy upon my soul as well.

The two of us stared at the ghostly embers that the fire had become. The Native American looked at me and spoke his final words. "The fire has gone out. The day of resurrection and the day of judgment are near. The constraints of time are finally starting to pass into eternity." I had no idea how much time had passed since I passed through death.

Ever so slowly, the odd, tingling sensation of feeling that I thought I had forgotten began to come over my spirit. I looked at my arms and legs. They were no longer ghostly traces, but a physical body was growing over my soul. Beginning with my fingers and toes, and crawling its extension over my hands and feet, and then over my arms, legs, and body, a radiant skin crept over me. I felt the graceful beating of my heart sending the pulse of blood through my body once more. I squeezed my right arm with my left hand and squeezed my left arm with my right hand. I reached up and touched my face and ran my fingers through my hair.

Light began to penetrate through the darkness, filling the cave with spectacular beauty. Suddenly there was no cave, but only the brilliant brightness of the sun and the most intense blue sky I had ever viewed. I breathed in deeply, experiencing the fresh air of the crisp earth, giving my lungs and my body and my muscles life. I could nearly taste the sweetness of the air after it had been so long since I inhaled it in. I saw with my physical eyes the absolute beauty of green forests, clear streams, blue oceans, and stony mountains.

And I realized the goodness that the physical realm was intended to be and the goodness that the physical realm had been remade into.

Before me, and seated on a throne, was a figure with a crown on his head. It was the King that the Native American had spoken of. The King looked into my eyes and at once my heart began to beat rapidly. Straightaway I was conscious that the King knew everything, good and evil, which I had done in life. All my actions, thoughts, and motives flooded before my eyes as I began to weep, experiencing a consuming love which I had never known before. The King was looking into my heart, examining me, and judging the condition of my spirit. I did not know what the King's decision would be, for as I saw my life's existence before my soul plunged into the shadowy depths of what some called Sheol and what others called Hades, I realized that I had been selfish more than I had been selfless, and I saw the great pains and evils that my selfishness had caused the people around me in life.

I dropped to my knees, for I honestly knew that in the King's justice I had been found guilty before him. I looked beside me to see if the Native American and the pirate were near, but there was no one else.

In one final plea before he passed his judgment, I asked the King for mercy to restore me to a life in love.

—

This is where the story of what is known of the man's life, death, resurrection, and judgment ends. Not even I, the author, can tell you what the King's final decision was regarding the condition of the man's heart and whether the man passed into eternal life or eternal damnation. Nor do I know the fate of the Native American or the pirate, for it is solely the King who, in both justice and mercy, can accurately examine and judge their hearts, as well as the hearts of any other individuals.

—

May God have mercy on both the living and the dead.

May God give us the wisdom to embrace the beauty of love in this life that we have before any of us cross over the river Styx and into death.

Antietam

1 Kings 12:24

"Thus says the LORD, You shall not go up or fight against your kindred the people of Israel. Let everyone go home, for this thing is from me." So they heeded the word of the LORD and went home again, according to the word of the LORD.

—

My own humanity, or whatever remained of it, was rejecting even this scant, stale piece of bread in its disgust of the scar that my life was becoming. Maybe by focusing on this food in between my depressed fingers, fingers that no longer had any strength or desire in them, and fingers dirtied with the bitter blood of dying men, my own disgusted mind might be distracted from the muscle contractions that gripped my abdomen with each wave of constant passing pain. It was not pain from illness; no, I had not been physically sick in weeks. Nor, solely by the sheer grace of God, was it the sharp, piercing pain of a wound sustained in battle; I had survived the day without being stabbed, shot, cut, or anything exploding into me. Though when the sun rose early this morning, its faint light finally burning through the ugly fog that futilely attempted to hide our sickening atrocities from our own traumatized eyes, it revealed the truth of the massacre we had caused to one another. Stumbling over the torn and tattered blue and grey wool of stiffened corpses piled upon each other, looking into empty eyes frozen in fear at their moment of death, and splashing through stagnant puddles of mud darkened with the deep crimson of slaughter, I desperately wanted to be one of those who was shot or stabbed. Those wounds would heal; that pain might one day disappear.

No, this was a pain that I did not believe would ever leave my agonized body. It was a pain that would someday numb my heart into death, and it was a pain that I would carry with me to judgment before God. It was a pain that only God in his mercy could remove from the shell that my heart would become because of this day that I wished I did not survive. It was a pain that started to defile my soul from the first day I said I would agree to kill another, and it was a pain that had finally run its course in hollowing out my humanity from the worm that grew inside.

I looked at my hand, now clenched in a fist of anger over the vile animals that this war had turned us into. The Union had their reasons and the Confederacy had their reasons. But the Congressmen and the Senators and the President were not the ones dying on a field, gasping for hopeless last breaths in anguish as they drowned in their own blood, spitting and coughing it up through broken teeth, trying in vain to say a message that could be passed on to their wife, son, or daughter. The Congressmen, Senators, and President were not the people holding the sweaty hands of these young men who looked at you with scared yet still courageous eyes that were striving to fight back tears one last time. They were not the ones telling them that it was going to be okay when there was, in fact, nothing that could be done to save their lives.

I opened my hand; the bloodied bread was crushed, useless to eat. I dropped it to the wet, reddened ground, a distaste in my mouth for the horrors of what people would do to one another.

The young man's dying face seared itself into what would most likely become the ever persistent but pestilent memory of this day; this would be a day that I knew no matter how much whiskey I drank, it would never fade from my recollection. I knew I would wake up years from now, sweating, with my wife sleeping next to me and asking me what was wrong, with the face of this child haunting my dreams and embodying the pain that would eternally tear away at my being. He could not have been older than 18; he may have been wearing the grey of the Confederacy, but he probably did not even truly understand why he was fighting.

Our ranks marched, one toward the other, getting closer and closer with each step through the grass. The sun cast down its light upon us in the heat of the day, our bodies trapped in the wool uniforms, soaking the cloth with sweat, as we took nervous breaths while our hearts thumped vigorously in our uneasy chests. My eyes wandered to the faces of the men across from us, not even fifty feet away. The same fear of death was just as much in their eyes as it was in ours. Our bayonets were fixed, the blades sharpened and ready to drive through the flesh of another with a killing stab. Someone began to run, his weapon pointed toward the people we were told to call our enemy. The rest of us followed, the soldiers of the Confederacy charging toward the soldiers of the Union and the soldiers of the Union charging toward the soldiers of the

Confederacy. Somewhere in my mind the thought of a preacher screaming about the evils of the South surfaced. Adrenaline surged through my body and my eyes filled with rage. I lowered my weapon and pointed the bayonet toward my countrymen, prepared to destroy the life of another human.

And then I saw the eyes of this young man. He was scared. He was terrified. The rage in my eyes paused for a moment as my humanity temporarily attempted to save me from what I was about to do.

And I continued to look at the shock that was consuming the expression on his face, his eyes wide but still staring directly into mine. His mouth was open, almost as if he wanted to ask me why, but he could not speak and could only take empty gulps of air. His knees fell to the ground as the boy simply fought to stay alive a few more moments. As I stared back at him, the Confederate boy dying at my own hands, my humanity briefly returned, also asking me the same question of why.

I wished that preacher could be here now, screaming about the evils of killing one another in war. Instead he is somewhere back home, safely north of the Mason-Dixon Line, standing behind the comfort of some pulpit as he yells at people who have no idea what is happening in the war they clamored for and who think that battle is some kind of romantic notion of honor. Evidently no one told them that human beings die in absolute misery here.

I am not even sure that God's angel of death would desire to be at the loathsome fields of Antietam. I can only pray that if this angel existed, he ushered all these dead soldiers into God's final presence of peace. Although God's peace will be the only thing that would possibly ever heal me, I do not yet know if I will ever allow myself to experience that grace. The face of that young man, that boy, would be my demonic reminder of the disgust of war, and the disgust of what I allowed myself to do in war.

I looked at the smashed piece of bread lying on the ground between my muddied, bloodied boots. A tear dropped to the ground next to it.

A sudden wave of crushing pain passed through my quivering chest, wrenching the callusing knot of what remained of my heart even tighter, before pressing its way through to my stomach and contracting my abdomen in its unrelenting grasp, making me gag excruciatingly painfully in its cruelty.

War, I thought to myself, *is pure stupidity.*

1 Kings 12

The smoke drifting through the dry desert air singed the hairs in my nostrils; a thin haze was spreading over the dusty trail leading to Bethel. The dirt, stomped on just long enough to grind it into a fine powder that was cast into the air with each footstep, mixed with the smoke; every breath of air was laced with the floating grime.

After glancing at my son walking next to me, I looked behind me to the multitudes of people stretching on for what were most likely thousands upon thousands of cubits. Everyone in the northern kingdom might as well have been on their way to Bethel. The smoke alone gave me a cough that persisted every few minutes; the dust kicked up by the people's feet made it worse. Holding my sleeve over my mouth, my son and I continued to walk, replacing the dirty smoke for the unpleasant stench of dirty sweat. When we started our journey, our garments were white; that was no longer the case. Streaks of dirt fused with layers of dust via hours of perspiration: it all accumulated over the days that we have been on the trail to Bethel. Nonetheless, we were getting close to the golden calf, the destination where we would finally offer our sacrifice; the smoke was a sure sign.

King Jeroboam issued the decree weeks ago. Honestly, I was relieved; it meant no more trips to Jerusalem. Bethel was less than a week's journey; the slow walk to Jerusalem with an animal sacrifice was another week after that. Many of my neighbors felt the same sense of relief. David, the priest in our village from the tribe of Levi, and who was also named after the great King, was not thrilled about Jeroboam's proclamation. David and I had conversations with one another at the market where my son and I traded figs and other fruits to support our family. David, who most people, but not everyone, loved, always visited our small stand. He regularly ended our conversations with the same question: "Have we forgotten our commandments already?" When he said those words, my heart beat a little more nervously; I did not want to recognize it, but David was right. I knew every word of the commandments; we were all taught them from the very day we came out of our mothers' wombs: we should never worship anyone besides the one true God, nor should there be any idols made of the one true God. David knew that the golden calf was a false god and an idol.

But the truth was that I did not want to make the trek to Jerusalem. Bethel was too close; it was convenient. I would not have to spend extra days away from my wife. My son and I could come back to the market sooner and harvest the fruit; it would be much better for our family. The fresh air seasoned with sweet, ripe, sugary figs seized my mind, even in the midst of Bethel. In the end, King Jeroboam's decision to move the sacrifices here made sense for everyone. David could gripe if he wanted to; my family and I were not complaining. It would not be that big of a deal to disregard these commandments in such a small way if it meant more time at home with my family and our business. I was sure the one true God would understand.

I took in another deep breath as I thought of the fresh air and fig trees, momentarily losing track of where my son and I actually were. I coughed into my sleeve as the aroma of burning acacia wood and the stench of smoking animal carcasses caught the back of my throat. People pushed on us from all sides, yet my son and I could not go anywhere. At least the smoke neutralized the sweaty odor of the plethora of people; without it I am not sure my son and I would have lasted long enough to make it to the golden calf. It was just enough to mask the smell of everyone traveling with their livestock.

A sheep blurted behind me. I jerked around, startled out of my daydream, and looked at the animal. There was not a single flaw on it. The sheep's owner slowly looked up at me; he was an old man with a wrinkled face, furrowed eyebrows, and deep brown eyes that stared right through me. I shuddered before I turned away, bringing my sleeve up to cover my mouth once more. *Where would a man even find a sheep without blemish? Why would he bring that sheep here for sacrifice? He could make so much money selling it in the market! So much quality wool for one animal!* The man was making a mistake in bringing his best sheep to the golden calf for sacrifice. I was about to turn around on the trail once again to say something to him, but immediately thought better of it when I remembered the man's old, piercing, cold eyes, furrowed brow, and wrinkled face.

In front of us was another man, also with his son. They had a small cow; there was not a single spot on it. After turning to my son, I looked down at our own pathetic looking sheep. I had second thoughts about the animal we brought to sacrifice; we had better quality sheep at home, almost as pure as the sheep that the old man had behind us. I rationalized to myself: *if it was Jerusalem we would have brought our best, but this is only Bethel and a golden calf. It won't matter here. It's only an idol.*

I took another step forward on what was now an even slower moving trail. The golden calf must be getting closer. The smoke was thicker and the foul smell of burning carcasses was stronger. I could barely breathe it in; I glanced at my son again to make sure he had something over his mouth. *Maybe Jerusalem would have been better after all*, I thought to myself.

Suddenly the quick glimmer of the reflection of the sun off something large and metallic caught my eye. I put my hand above my eyes and tried to make out what could have caught the sun's rays so strongly; it might have been a trader's clanging pots and pans or another merchant's iron tools of his trade. Amongst the drifting shouts of the throngs of people, plenty of metallic rings broke through noise. After we made the sacrifice to the golden calf, I decided I would find one of the merchants and barter for a new metal pan.

The bright reflection in the distance was neither pots nor pans nor tools. Grabbing my son's shoulder, I pointed to the object, both of us still covering our mouths with our sleeves from our free hands. The smell of the people and the animals was almost unbearable. The smoke was not doing such a good job anymore of hiding the reek of animal sacrifices. Before the smoke had that small benefit; now it was purely a nuisance. *Jerusalem has a much better operation set up for the sacrificial system*, I thought. David really was right. I shouldn't have been complaining so much, though; I was the one who wanted to come to Bethel after all.

It was the golden calf, less than a thousand cubits away. The bright sunlight reflecting off the large structure made it incredibly difficult to look at, even through the haze; the gold only magnified the full intensity of the sun in every direction. But it was beautiful. I quickly forgot the smoke and the burning carcasses and the crowds of people talking and shouting; even my son and my wife and the fresh air scented with ripe figs abandoned my mind. All I could think of was the beauty of the idol of the golden calf. Bethel was worth it. I did not want to go back to Jerusalem and its temple again. Here I could see the god that we were sacrificing to; there I could not see the god and the priests handled everything. I could survive the horrid conditions of sacrificing at Bethel if it meant seeing the golden calf every year.

—

Then I stepped in it. Before I could stop myself, and before I realized what the small blemish free cow in front of me just did on the trail, and before my nose caught the disgusting scent of what the man's livestock just did, my right foot landed in the nauseating pile of excrement lying in the middle of the trail to Jeroboam's golden calf of Bethel. I almost vomited in the sleeve I was holding up to cover my mouth. *Jerusalem would have been so much better.*

David, the priest from my small village, would have said I deserved it; he would have been right.

The Fall of Belshazzar

The drug runner removed his right index finger from the trigger of the pistol he was holding to the sailboat captain's head. The captain continued to stare back at the man, unsure of what was happening, but the trafficker's gaze was now turned up towards the clear night sky.

A slight breeze swept across the open water, but it was not enough to push any significant waves across the black sea's surface. The sailing vessel stayed level in the international waters off the coast of south Florida, nearly still on the dark water. There were no other lights visible; they were alone out there – a sailing captain and a couple of his crew and a drug runner and a couple of his crew. When they gave the sailboat captain the coordinates of where to hand off the drug shipment coming in from South America, the cartel wanted to ensure that they would all be in the middle of nowhere.

The captain had never done anything like this before; he had been threatened by the cartel to carry the drugs on his boat. Their messenger, a short man with a deep scar on his right cheek, told him that he would only have to bring in this single shipment and he would not be bothered again; he said it with a sickening smile on his face. He pointed a pistol at the captain and his crew as a few men, also with weapons, loaded several boxes inside the cabin. After the captain left the port, asking himself how this could happen, he realized that the cartel had been observing him for some time, and they knew that his boat would make the perfect vessel to smuggle their drugs to the United States. It would not have been difficult for someone to figure out that the captain chartered sailing trips all over the Caribbean and Gulf of Mexico. No one would suspect him. But now that he and his two crew members had been forced into the operation, the captain realized that there would not be a good way out of the situation.

—

The captain was nervous. He gave his crew the signal to shut off the engines once they reached the coordinates. They only became aware of the unconscious comfort brought by the hum of the motor when it suddenly disappeared. They waited in the silent darkness; if anything went wrong, there would be no help.

His heart pounded quickly. Sweat formed across his brow. He loosely held the wheel in front of him, his hand starting to shake as his nerves began to take control of his mind and body. The twitching of his hand, the increased sweat on his forehead, the surging pulse of his heart – they all magnified as he, without realizing it, allowed fear to take him further to the edge of suffering from his growing anxiety.

He looked down at his trembling hand. He gripped the wheel of the boat and took in several deep breaths of the cool night Gulf air. Taking out the small silver flask of whiskey he kept in his jacket, the captain unscrewed the top and took a drink before sliding it back in to his pocket. It was a habit he was not proud of, but he decided he would not quit tonight.

A light appearing in the distance grew larger as the sound of a small powerboat speeding toward his sailboat intensified. The captain nodded to his two crew members, letting them know that it was the drug runners from the cartel. The captain, worried for their safety, sternly instructed his crew to stay out of the way once they met up with the traffickers.

The powerboat pulled up next to them; one of the three men in the powerboat threw a rope onto the deck of the sailboat. The other two jumped onto the sailboat and tied the two boats together. One of the men, probably the one in charge, pulled out his pistol and waved for the other two sailboat crew members to stand by the captain. Meanwhile, the other two traffickers went into the cabin to remove the boxes that the cartel hid in the boat when they left the port. The sailing captain continued to stare at their leader, who still had his pistol pointed at them. He wondered if this was normal for a cartel's smuggling operation, or if this meant that the captain and his sailboat were only needed one time.

The two men finished bringing out the boxes from the cabin and hid them in their powerboat. Their leader raised his pistol, pointing it directly at the head of the captain, and placed his right index finger on the trigger. He showed no emotion as the captain looked back into his cold, dark eyes. The captain took a breath. Fear still pulsed through his body, but in what he realized would be his last moments, he showed strength in the face of death.

The drug runner glanced towards the star-filled sky; something above him caught his attention. All at once, his cold eyes widened as he opened his mouth, taking a sudden breath.

—

The captain returned to his quarters, eager to forget about what just happened. He took out the bottle of whiskey he kept in the cabinet by his bed along with a small glass, and poured himself a shot of the burning liquid. He set the glass and the bottle down on the table next to his bed as he took a seat, thinking about how close he had come to death. He wondered what the drug runner could have seen in the sky that prompted this criminal, this man who would have otherwise not thought twice about killing him and his crew, to become so visibly shaken up that he put down his gun and left the sailboat without saying a single word.

He picked up his glass and walked back outside to the deck, where he ran into both of his crew leaning against the small railing.

"Some night, Captain."

"Yeah. I'd say so. I'm sorry for bringing you both into this."

"It's not like we had a choice, Captain. If we refused, they would have killed us anyway and just taken our boat. These people don't care about our lives." The crew member paused. "But you ever see anything like that before?"

The captain was confused for a moment. They had just been in the middle of a drug smuggling operation that nearly cost them their lives. Of course he had never seen anything like that before! It was an odd question for one of his crew to be asking, considering the circumstances.

"What do you mean?"

"The writing in the sky. I've never seen anything like it. One moment it was there, being written, and the next moment it was gone. But that drug runner saw it. It was what spooked him. It probably saved our lives."

The captain became even more confused. Evidently the smuggling was not the strangest thing that occurred that evening.

"Writing in the sky? What did it say?"

"I really don't know what the words meant, but the words were being written out in cursive, almost as if someone was writing them in real time, you know? Something, or someone, wrote, '*Mene mene tekel parsin.*' Some sort of foreign language maybe."

The captain thought for a minute before smiling and taking a deep, relaxing breath, inexplicably relieved to hear the news his crew gave him. The captain remembered his childhood and one of the stories his parents told him. He had not yet drunk the whiskey in his cup; he looked down at it as it swirled around, the captain moving the glass in a small slow circular motion with his hand.

"What do you think it means, Captain?"

A few more seconds passed. He turned the glass upside down, letting the whiskey fall into the Gulf of Mexico seawater. His crew looked at him, somewhat surprised.

"It means that – the idiot who held a gun to my head – his days are numbered. And they are. I buried a GPS tracker in their drug shipment and radioed the U.S. Coast Guard." The captain paused briefly before finishing his thought. "And it also means that the cartel's empire will fall."

The captain surveyed the quiet sea with confidence, before looking up towards the clear night sky where the words were written shortly before. He turned to his two crew members. "It's a beautiful night to be alive."

The Ammonite Messenger

Nehemiah squinted his eyes as he scanned the far reaches of the horizon. The small outline of a man riding a horse appeared, silhouetted against the reddening sky. The rider was still a good distance away; if it was not for the setting sun casting shadows over the landscape, Nehemiah would have been able to see the entire expanse clearly in the dry air.

The horse kicked up a cloud of dust as the rider disappeared below the horizon, blurring the sharp contrast between him and the sinking red desert sun. Nehemiah faintly discerned their shape racing toward them among the shadows. They were at the borders of what was, to Nehemiah's ancestors, once the northern kingdom; it was now divided between various pagan rulers as the conquering Persians split up their territories. First the Assyrians swept over the land, then the Babylonians, and then the Medes, and then the Persians. The Babylonians transported much of the southern kingdom's population back to their capital and into diaspora; the Persians, generations later, allowed the exiles to finally return to their home.

Nehemiah, serving in the court of the Persian King Artaxerxes, petitioned the ruler to allow him to return to the land of his ancestors in order to rebuild Jerusalem. The King even gave Nehemiah, along with the others going with him, several of his prized Persian horses for their journey home. The Babylonians and the Persians, extending their empire to the west, brought many more of these exceptional animals with them into the area.

The pounding hooves thundered closer. "Halt," the rider yelled. "Halt!" The horse, a large, black, muscled beast, finally stopped in front of Nehemiah and the others. The trail of settling dust stretched all the way back to the horizon; the bottom edge of the sun was just beginning to dip below it. "You are now in the land of Ammon. By order of the governor of the land, Tobiah the Ammonite, installed by the Persian king himself, you must make yourself known!"

Nehemiah did not speak a word, but looked sternly at the rider from atop his own horse. He knew that the surrounding provinces would not like the idea of Jerusalem's restoration. And even despite Artaxerxes' blessing, Nehemiah realized that the bordering territories would do everything they could to stop them. They did not want to see the walls of Jerusalem rebuilt.

Nehemiah reached into the pouch beside him and pulled out a piece of parchment. As he handed the letter to the man on the black horse, the rider recognized Artaxerxes' seal. Lifting it up to catch the remaining sunlight so that he could read, the man began to speak.

"To the governors of the province Beyond the River; to Sanballat the Horonite; to Tobiah the Ammonite; to Asaph the Keeper of the King's Forest:

"My servant Nehemiah has served with much honor in my court as my cupbearer. He has asked me to allow him to return to the land of his ancestors to rebuild their city of

Jerusalem. Because he has demonstrated nothing but great loyalty to me, I have granted him this request."

The rider stopped reading out loud and studied the remainder in silence. Nehemiah continued to look at the man as the sunlight waned.

A minute later, the rider stopped reading the parchment. He had a disgusted, almost angry, look on his face.

"It appears you have done well for yourself in Artaxerxes' court, Nehemiah. The King's favor is upon you and this little project of yours. I hope you know that, because his favor is going to be the only favor you will get. Tobiah the Ammonite will grant you safe passage through his land, but you will get nothing else from him. And you will not get any help from Sanballat the Horonite either. Whether you have this letter or not, we do not want you Jews rebuilding Jerusalem. We will do everything we can to stop it from happening. We will wage war against you if it comes to it. Try to move one stone in place and we will attack." The rider paused, shoving the letter back into Nehemiah's open hand. "Go back to Artaxerxes, Nehemiah. We do not want you here. Your people do not even want you here."

The Ammonite messenger, unhappy about the prospect of Jerusalem being rebuilt, picked up the reins of his black horse and pulled them to the side. The horse snorted as it reared its head back. The rider slapped the reins down and the horse bolted off in the direction the messenger came from. Nehemiah watched the man disappear over the horizon in a cloud of dust, taking the last of the red sun with him behind the skyline.

One of the men with Nehemiah turned to him in the fading light. "What will we do Nehemiah?"

"What will we do? We will arm the people building the walls! Jerusalem will be rebuilt. We have no need to fear pagan rulers and their threats. They worship powerless idols while we worship the true God."

Nehemiah leaned forward, placing his hand at the base of the horse's mane. He and the others moved forward, beginning their trek through the hostile land as they continued their journey to Jerusalem.

Luke 9:23

In memory of David

—

The voices in the hallway faded as the volunteers walked past Nathan's office and made their way towards the kitchen. Every Tuesday, they came in to help prepare the dinner at the shelter. There was a knock at the door a few minutes after the volunteers passed.

"Come in," Nathan stated. He looked up from his desk. It was Bill. "You can leave the door open." Bill looked anxious as he sat down.

"You know – some days are worse than other days; I don't know what it is. I guess today is just one of those tough days," Bill stated.

"What's going on?" Nathan asked. Bill stared at the ground for an instant before shaking his head.

Bill forced a laugh. "Some days you wake up and you just want a drink. I know." Bill attempted to smile before he took a deep breath. "I know – I shouldn't want it, but I wake up in the morning and that temptation is there. Nothing I can do about it." Nathan nodded as he listened to Bill share his story. "You know – when I was in prison, it wasn't really that bad. I behaved well and was rewarded for it. I only went there because I was stupid. I made a really stupid mistake that I should've never done in the first place."

Bill thought about his life before looking up at Nathan, his eyes still serious. "It was really just greed that landed me there. In a way, it's almost a good thing I was caught; I mean, who knows if I would've turned into an alcoholic or not if I hadn't been caught, but I would've definitely been pretty far lost down the path of greed." Bill stopped before forcing another chuckle. "But then I started drinking when I got out. I just got so depressed. Then I kept drinking." Bill tried to force another smile and looked straight at Nathan. "Well, you know the rest of the story! I entered this recovery program here. Then I quit once. And now I'm back again!" Bill let out more laughter.

Nathan waited another couple moments before speaking.

"I've got no doubt that it's tough, Bill. But you're doing a great job. Don't forget that. Every day is a fresh start. Every time you've got that temptation to grab a drink, you've got a choice. And you can choose to say no." Nathan took a breath. "You've seen where alcohol has taken you. It might feel good at first, but it won't lead you anywhere good. You might have to say no to that desire every single day. But you've got a choice to say no. And you've got a choice to put that instinct within you to death every single day. The great thing is – you don't have to say yes. It may never be easy; the temptation may never go away. But every time you wake up and have that thirst for a drink, you can still say no." Bill grinned at Nathan's words.

"God. Being sober sucks." Bill shifted in his chair; it was clear that he still had more on his mind. Nathan waited for him to speak again. "It does suck. You know – I believe in myself.

Some days more than others, but I do believe in myself. And I know God believes in me." Bill became solemn. "But when I walk around town, like yesterday, and I see how some people look at me. Some of them knew how horrible of a drunk I was. I know they remember me stumbling around like some pathetic loser. You know – I stood out in front of that financial firm downtown. I panhandled, hoping some of those rich guys walking out each afternoon would be able to spare some cash. You'd be surprised. A lot of them would give and a lot of them wouldn't." Bill stopped again as he reflected. "I'm just not sure that I believe that other people believe in me. I'm not sure people think I can really change after everything."

As soon as Bill said those words, Nathan recalled Williamson Financial Investments. It was the firm where he used to work. Although Nathan was a little older now, he held a position there for practically his entire life. Nathan vaguely remembered a bearded man, probably homeless, who stood outside his office for a while. Then one day the man simply disappeared; Nathan never thought anything of it. It might've even been Bill, but Nathan couldn't call to mind the details of the man's face. He searched his memory. Nathan remembered how he was back then though; he probably tried to walk past the bearded man as quickly as he could.

"Bill, you already said it. You believe in yourself. You should believe in yourself every day! And you know that God believes in you. That's all that matters." Nathan leaned forward. "Look at me, Bill; I want you to know just how serious I am. I know that other people believe in you. I believe in you. You're making progress. I've seen you make progress. And the rest of the staff here at the shelter believe in you. There is no need to worry about anyone who might doubt you." Nathan paused before reclining back in his chair. "You never shared that part of your story with me before, about your panhandling. Thanks for that. Regardless if people change or not, I just have to place faith in the hope that they do." Nathan looked at Bill in the eyes. "But I happen to think that people really can change. That's why I'm here."

Bill considered Nathan's words before grinning again. This time the smile wasn't forced. "You know – you're right!" Bill stood up and began to head towards the office door. "Thanks Nate, I really mean it. I know I come in here and tell you the same story every week, but it really does make a difference that someone is listening."

"You'll be fine, Bill."

"I know."

As Bill left, Nathan heard a few others in the hallway again. Some of the volunteers who came in for the afternoon to help prepare the dinner were on their way out.

"Hey Nate, we'll all see you next time!" It was one of the volunteers named Sarah. She stopped in and chatted with Nathan every once in a while.

"Sounds great!" Nathan replied. Sarah's daughter stopped and waved from the hallway.

"Goodbye, Mr. Williamson!" Nathan smiled at the girl and waved back.

Babble, Part Two

The clouds covered the sun, an attempt to block the light from breaking into the mid-day darkness. The air, cooled in the dim shadows of the veiled sky, was heavy with the weight of death's perpetual process.

The hawk, a distant relative of Oph, soared high above the outskirts of the desert town. Its eyes turned upwards towards the glowing star above him, hazy as it struggled to make its reappearance. Though the hawk could not recognize it, an echo of eternity was slowly beginning to resonate across the core of its own being. It was a distant ripple of a wave that, at its origin, and like a child throwing a stone into a murky pond, began its surge in the man beneath him. The hawk flapped its wings and turned its gaze downwards, scanning the hill below him.

The hawk, always quick to find the scent of a life nearing its end, had already followed this man earlier in the day; the man labored as he climbed the hill, stopping every few moments to rest as he carried a burden that seemed to weigh more than the world itself. He left drops of his blood on the trail behind him, drying in the dust, as the crowd following him trampled on that blood with their footsteps.

The hawk spread his wings and soared down, circling closer to the dying man. Death was near for him. The women by the man wept as they looked at his broken body.

The hawk landed on a perch next to the man. He struggled to breathe; his arms were outstretched and he could not move them, preventing him from drawing in the air around him. The man turned his head toward the hawk. The man's eyes, which revealed pain yet also showed mercy, met with the small unknowing eyes of the hawk. An echo of the past beat within the hawk's heart.

The man turned to look at the people below him. He closed his chapped lips and attempted to swallow, but no saliva came to his dry mouth. Someone below him laughed.

The man said several words, but the hawk could not understand. The two men being crucified next to him looked at the man between them. The hawk knew, instinctively, who death would visit first.

The hawk again flapped its wings, taking off from his perch, climbing through the air, circling, and waiting for death to take its course.

The clouds above, gathered in darkness and shutting out the sun, issued a single deep, lasting cry of thunder.

The hawk circled above the hill once more, scanning the earth below him. Again, a faint chord of eternity sounded within the hawk's being. The man below him was dead.

—

The first light of the rising sun cast its rays onto a small purple flower growing outside the small cave. The fading night was starting its daily retreat from the advancing day. The air, so easily chilled in the dry darkness, was ready to escape the shadows and warm itself in the brightness of the morning sun.

The hawk, a distant relative of Yaphah, flapped her wings as she landed on a small tree just above the cave. The tree, which had not birthed any green leaves for years, was beginning to bud as it sensed a new urgency towards life. Though the hawk could not recognize it, an echo of the same spirit which spurred the dead tree to grow leaves was beginning to plant itself within her own heart. Eternity was breaking into the constraints of death with which time is measured, this same grip of death which had broken the world around the hawk and the tree so long ago.

The hawk, always curious to discover something new, had followed the two women as they traveled in the moonlight to this small cave on the outskirts of the desert town. With them, they carried packages in their arms. The hawk, who could always sense vibrant life, did not discern it within these two women. The women, mourning the death of a friend, left drops of their tears in the dusty trail as they walked. Yet the hawk, always alert to the world around it, perceived no death in this place.

The hawk spread her wings and quickly flew to another rock below the small tree, giving her a clear view of the cave. It was empty. The hawk heard the dull thuds of packages of spices dropping to the ground. A rock was rolled to the side; it was not simply a cave, but a tomb. The thundering cry of a moving boulder had already been issued from the earth even before the hawk and the women arrived.

A man dressed in white appeared before the women. He glanced at the hawk behind them. Eternity shined from deep within his eyes; the man was a messenger from a place that was beyond the boundaries of time. The two women, shocked, muttered inaudibly, and shook nervously before this man.

The man gave them a message. The hawk could not understand the words that the man said, but the voice spoke of an event beyond the mere descriptive capabilities of syllabic constructs. The event that the messenger was talking about reflected into her heart a distant memory of the joy that the world once was and a vision of a hope of what the world will soon become.

The two women turned away, surprise and uncertainty on their faces. The hawk knew, instinctively, that there was no need to fear uncertainty. The ripples that had affected the heart of her friend a few days ago had strengthened into waves of hope which were starting to weave themselves into every aspect of her existence.

The messenger looked at the hawk once again and smiled. The man who had been in the tomb was no longer there; in the midst of death, the man who was once in the tomb brought life into the world. The hawk turned for a moment, looking back up at the tree above the tomb. It had grown full leaves, vivid, lush, and green.

The hawk turned its head back to the man dressed in white. He was gone, revealing the purple flower that was growing behind him. The hawk flapped her wings again, taking off, rising into the sky, life pulsing through her body as she scanned the earth below her.

Across an Ocean

For the broken-hearted.

—

I stood there. Shallow waves collided with the gravel and the sand at the edge of the water as the ever moving grey, blue, and green expanse ahead of me faded into a hazy line, the only separation from the clear blue sky above. Staring out towards that horizon, I wondered, asking myself if it was worth it. My thoughts were about as focused as the void of ocean and sky I was looking at; one day they seemed content only to be churned the next day into restlessness by the wind and waves.

At my feet was a seaworthy kayak. Perhaps the boat, half on the beach and half in the ocean, bobbing up and down with the incoming waves, was symbolic of the hesitation within my mind. But in deciding to get in that small vessel, I knew there would only be one direction to go. Across that great expanse, that void which would soon contain only water, sky, me, and maybe the gods, was a girl far beyond the horizon. Part of my heart was with her, and chances were she did not even realize just how much of my heart was there.

It seemed simple enough: myself, a boat, a paddle, and a body of water to work my way across. Humanity had conquered water before. People sailed around the world. The Vikings traversed the Atlantic in wooden ships. People had even kayaked across oceans and lived to tell the tale. Even I had paddled hundreds of miles over water in just a matter of days. But here one paddle stroke forward was a slow chip off the possible thousands of miles that remained. I had no idea how long it would take me. Maybe what remained of my heart would give way before I would even be halfway and I would simply float, dehydrated and on the brink of death, hungry sharks in my lingering wake. But the rest of my heart was on the other side of that sea which separated myself and her, this water the only connection between the very land each of us walked on.

I looked down at my empty boat once again and made a decision. That connection which was seemingly unending, a connection which many would not even dare to venture across, the very thought of which screamed impossible, I would cross. I took one last look into the distance. The blue sky above me and the vast ocean in front of me did not end. The weather today was warm with no clouds in sight; the wind would be at my back pushing me eastward. Looking down, the beach submerged below the water, forming that symbolic line I needed to cross. I knelt down, my leg against the smooth yet still grating and finite crystals. Grabbing a handful of sand, I let it run through my fingers and back to the earth. This would be a journey into the unknown. And while I knew that I would once again be able to allow that sand to run through my fingers when I completed this journey, my broken heart might finally begin to be repaired when I once again had earth beneath my feet.

—

The splash of a low wave gently tapping the bow of my boat against the steady drip of salt water running down the blade of my paddle and back into the ocean had become the constant rhythm of the music my ears were now accustomed to. Every so often, the call of a seagull swooping, or the cry of another bird of prey diving through the air and crashing through the surface, or the occasional fish jumping in the distance, added to that rhythm.

All around me the surface of the sea sparkled, small crystals forming at the peaks of waves and reflecting sunlight across the surface. The light breeze blew the smell of saltwater in all directions. I had not seen anyone in days. It may have been a week since I left that beach; I was not sure. To tell the truth, I did not truly care. Based on the sun in the day and the stars during the night, I knew which direction I needed to go. My only goal was to put my paddle in the water and move forward in the slow rise and fall of the waves surrounding me. If anything was going to stop me, it would not be the physical torment; no, that would only be temporary. I could see an end to that. And even so, the determination of the human mind can continue on even when the body is weakened. Even with all of that, the only thing that might defeat me would be a spirit broken by the separation between myself and this girl who was still so far away. Anything the wind and the waves threw at me would only weaken me, but not defeat me.

Those first several days, it seemed that if there was a god out there, he had blessed me in my effort. The wind at my back created swells in the water, propelling me forward every few minutes. And while the sun continued to shine down, the temperature was just right; it was neither too hot nor too cold. But I knew that the sea could not be trusted forever. It was a predator lying in wait. It did not need to stalk, for it already surrounded anything it would swallow. But I knew that the day would come soon when it would begin to mock me with its power, and then a day after that when it would stop toying with me and simply use its power to stop me. I was mentally preparing for that day, but in the meantime, I would take advantage of the weather I had been blessed with. I returned my gaze to the prisms within the crests of the considerate swells the ocean was giving me.

—

Her eyes were like those prisms trapped in the peaks of ocean waves. Each wave caught the sun's rays and cast them out in every direction in a brilliance which one could not stare at for long. Looking into her eyes, there was the complexity of a puzzle of an infinite kaleidoscope calling out with a radiant spark of love which reflected the deep life within her. It was mesmerizing. And like the ocean, those waves were only the surface of an unfathomable mystery. Scientists and researchers were beginning to gain some understanding of the life that existed under the ocean's surface, but there will always be the unknown. A girl's eyes are the same; they are a beautiful glimpse into that unknown, into the depth that is her life. They only begin to shed light on the mystery of who she is, and there was no limit to wondering about her once I began to look at her eyes. Somehow I knew I was searching for an answer that would never be found as I gazed at the colors of her irises before settling into the darkness of her pupils that were the entrance to her very being.

—

The day had come. The patient monster beneath the deceptive surface was slowly beginning to lift its head after attempting to bring me into a false sense of security. The waves' crests no longer reflected the beauty they had contained just a few days ago, but instead formed an uneasy feeling within me as the encroaching clouds began to cast a dark shadow over the growing swells. It would be an ominous forecast for the remainder of my journey. I put my head down and prepared for whatever this great body of water might do in its ever changing whims.

It was the choice I had made and a journey that I must finish. It was me against whatever gods of the ocean and sky were out there, battling through their elements in order to reach the shores of a distant land in my quest to heal my heart. The sky darkened as the rain weighted the clouds down, bridging the gap between ocean and sky as the water in each yearned for reunification. As I turned my head to look at the distance behind me, I could see the sun pushing its last rays of warmth through a thin layer of clouds down to any remaining life on the surface. I pushed my legs to the outside of the kayak, preparing to brace for the onslaught that would begin. Yet even though my heart sank as I sat there at the edge of the storm with the certain prospect of ensuing darkness, she was the bright spot that kept any hope alive.

Just as a child might push his or her hands together in a pond in an attempt to catch an elusive minnow, the dropping pressure only pushed the air between the clouds and the sea into a futile chase across the waves. Along its way, the howls caught stray splashes of waves and inevitably drove them in my direction. The wet sting of saltwater pelted my face every few seconds. Spray relentlessly assaulted the shell of what I hoped was an impenetrable kayak. And when it had no success against the boat, it began to penetrate through my clothes, driving into my body, soaking the shirt I was wearing. The wind only grew stronger; no matter which direction I paddled in, the ocean sneered at me with a headwind. The only direction I had any success in was backwards.

As the storm began settling into its rage above me, it sent gusts of swift wind across the surface just as an army sends in its initial forces. The god of the sea allied itself with the god of the sky in a game which the two were playing with my life; I was the helpless, bouncing puck and the game would only be finished when the ocean opened its gnashing, cold, wet teeth and I would finally be tossed in to score the goal. Ocean swells grew bigger as the storm flung its gales through the churning black and foaming mouth of the sea. Wave after wave pounded and slammed across the bow and stern of the kayak and my only weapon against them was the paddle in my hand. My only maneuver in this game that the two played with my life was defense as I struggled to brace against each impacting wave. I could only pray through the rise, fall, and plummeting crash of each swell as my stomach churned almost as violently as the sea I was on. To whom I was praying, I did not know; but flashes of the girl's beauty brought me moments of peace through the chaos around me.

The rain fell hard. The sting of saltwater battered me from all sides as beads of rain plummeted from the sky, only to be tossed and thrown much like myself on their plunge back to the ocean. The rain was cold, another bombardment from the dark and angry sky above. The tempest hurled curtains of water at me, giving shape to the wind and revealing its true form as it surrounded me with each advance. It could no longer hide its enraged fury as it unleashed the anger contained within the storm. The innocent droplets of rain now only served as more ammunition against any hope that I still carried.

The rolls of thunder deafened as the squall drew closer to the water, followed by the blinding and immediate flash of lightning. The deep cry of its fury raged across the darkness and through the clouds. Its echo could be heard as a warning to those who might still be foolish enough to hang around the storm's borders. And while I was the only one bold enough to confront this axis of sky and water, I only seemed to incense its wrath more when I continued in my refusal to surrender.

There we were in this maddening game of destruction between humanity and the gods of the ocean and the sky. They cursed me with their alliance as I cursed them in my dissent, both of us exasperated and out of breath in this clash. I sat there in the cockpit of my kayak, rolling with the continuing waves, looking towards the heavens, wondering if I could make this formidable beast above me give up in frustration. Cold, wet, and shivering, the wind cutting through my clothing and sending spasms through my nearly broken body and spirit, I had not given up yet. I was only weakened, but not defeated. I took in a deep breath, cleared my head if only for a moment, and contemplated my options.

This interminable foe would clearly overcome me if I continued to be a stubborn thorn in its side. Yet I had put up a stronger fight than it had planned for. I was not broken yet, but I knew if it carried on it would only be a matter of time. Maybe it would show mercy. Maybe it would recognize my persistent spirit. Maybe I had earned its respect just as these gods of the great blue wilderness had earned mine. And maybe it would see my heart, judge it accordingly, and allow me to continue this passage. I looked up toward the sky and wondered if it had heard my cry. Slowly I raised my arms and struggled to put the paddle blade in the water; I could only speculate on what the gods' response might be.

—

There was no blue sky ahead, only the dull grey darkness of clouds and rolling water. The wind and the waves slowed. They no longer plowed straight into my body in their attempt to run me over. The rain subsided. Stinging sheets of ice water no longer dropped from above. But the dim skies ahead were still dark. Maybe in some way the gods of the ocean and the sky had heard my pleas and this was their form of compassion and mercy. Or maybe their tactics had changed and they were placing bets on how long I could last without the hope of clear skies. The sun had not managed to break through the ominous shield of clouds since the first hints of foul weather on the horizon. A grey misery continued to hold its grip around me.

My sense of time was completely lost; the storm may have lasted a few days or a few weeks, but I had no idea. I came to the brink of defeat more than once during that squall, only to find a last few ounces of strength come from somewhere in my body to continue to push on toward survival. I paddled slower as I carried the wounds of the storm throughout my body, mind, and spirit. If there was only one thing that continued to give me hope through this despair, it was the idea that I would one day land on solid ground, find the girl that carried the other half of my heart, and be with her once again.

—

The girl's manner was just the opposite of the storm that had tossed me so carelessly between its waves. Her demeanor was peace. Unlike the fickle gods of the ocean and sky, who would give you solitude one moment and throw you into oblivion the next moment without a second of hesitation, a glance from this girl seemed as if it would calm any heart forever. Her peace, in the midst of this wild storm which had engulfed me as the ocean and sky hurled insults of defeat at me, was the only light I had in my darkness. It was all that enabled me to place the paddle in the water once more, even as the wind snaked its way around the waves in its attempt to entrap me in misery.

—

Inside me was a hollow knot that twisted with every echo as my stomach yearned for something to digest. I was hungry. I had hardly eaten anything over the course of the journey. During the rising storm I could barely keep anything down. All that had sustained me to this point were the occasionally ensnared bird or the sporadically caught fish. Even so, I probably would not be able to eat much more than the bare boned fish I was existing on.

The first few weeks I could hear the rumbles vibrating the walls of the cavern that my stomach had become. Eventually the grumbling dissipated only to be replaced by the indiscriminate pain of my stomach walls twisting in a shout to be fed. It was clear to me that I was losing weight. The gauntness of the meager fish and birds I ate was beginning to spread over me. My arms were an undernourished quandary of bones and muscle that was only getting leaner. My face probably looked the same, and I did not even want to look at my legs. This trip was taking its toll on my body. I had survived the raw wrath of the ocean's savage storm only weeks before without questioning my purpose, only to have the lingering and persistent voice of hunger give me doubts.

The surrounding seawater cast its salty stench in every direction. It was on the tip of my nose and the end of my tongue. Layers of fine white crystals accumulated on me not only from the splash of waves, but also from the sweat that dripped from my skin on the increasingly rarer warm days. Fishermen put their catch in tubs of salt to preserve their yield. People put salt on their food to add to the flavor. And city workers put salt on the roads to melt the ice and dry them out during the winter months. I felt as if I was the victim of all three. And the salt just sat there drying me out, parching my throat and nostrils as I breathed it in, slowly dehydrating me from both the inside and the outside. Even if I arrived to the sandy shores of my destination on the brink of death, at least I knew my body would be well preserved.

There was water all around me, taunting me with its infinite presence. Yet I could not drink any of it. As the salt slowly drained the remaining moisture from my body, all I desired was to take long gulps of fresh, crisp, and cool water. But the ocean had deceived me before and it would jump at the chance to play more tricks on a tired, weary, and dry mind. I had read too many stories of people lost at sea and what had happened to them once they finally succumbed to the temptation that the ocean gods placed before their eyes like a bountiful feast.

Hope was there but I struggled to hold on. I began to wonder who would win the bet the sky and ocean placed on my life. I even thought about what the winnings might be, but then realized my life was probably the prize. The two probably kept a scoreboard of how many halfwits they had defeated in their barren world.

—

There, walking across the water, was a person coming in my direction. I could not tell if it was a man or a woman. But behind the person were blue clouds and the sun's streaming light silhouetting the individual. My heart jumped and adrenaline forced its way through my rusty and salty veins, giving me energy I did not know I had. I had not seen blue skies or the sun's rays during what seemed like months of ridicule and jeers from the ocean and sky as they continued their attempt to break my spirit. I did not know if what I was seeing was real. Mentally, I was exhausted. Physically, my body was nearing collapse. Spiritually, I was a wreck. Emotionally, I was beyond fatigue. But I continued to look at what appeared to be a human being coming near me. The person did not say a single thing to me, but instead beckoned me toward them.

Peace began to fill my heart. Rest started to embrace my body. Hope once again made its way to my spirit. My emotions lifted as I saw this silhouette waving me closer. I asked myself if I was in a dream or if what remained of my heart had finally stopped and I had passed away in my sleep. If it was a dream I did not not want it to stop. If it was death then I did not want to return to life. The figure continued to wave me toward them almost as if they knew me.

Clarity began to return to my brain. I gripped the paddle in my hand and put the blades in the water as I felt the familiar yet resistant pull of water underneath me. This was no dream; it was reality. In that instant, I knew I was going to make it across the ocean. I knew I would once again have land beneath my feet. Blood pumped through my body as I continued to lift my arms. I took one more look around at the now all too familiar kayak I had been sitting in for too long; it looked different with the sun shining down on it. It looked like even the boat itself had hope. I drove my blade into the blue ocean water and propelled myself forward with ease as the kayak glided over the surface.

I did not see it coming, but a wave crashed over me. I did not know from which direction it came, but as the cool water dripped down my hair and over my face it did not have the taste of salt. Instead it was fresh, cold, clear, and crisp. It was the living water that I had searched and longed for, but never thought I would find. A fish jumped to my left and I heard the splash of another to my right. I looked behind me and a bird was sitting on the rear deck of my vessel. I glanced skyward and saw only the clouds in the far distance behind me. Again I looked ahead of me, wondering if the person would still be there. Instead the figure was gone. Blue sky remained. A breeze picked up at my back. And for the first time in months, I saw land ahead of me. It was time to celebrate! Whoever it was, they had brought true hope, peace, and restoration with them.

—

The last week in the boat went by slowly as I sat there, rising and falling with the swells, staring at the mass of earth before me. My mind wandered for hours, wondering what it would be like to feel sand between my toes once again and have it fall through my fingers. I asked myself if the land would attack me with a vendetta after I had left it for so long or if it would allow me to simply enjoy its presence in peace. I questioned if this floating sensation that has been ingrained within me would ever leave.

Days passed as the land on the horizon never seemed to get closer. But it was there, and no matter how painful it became to lift my deteriorating muscles and put the paddle in the water, I had the determination to keep going until the end. If a snail could swim, it would have probably moved faster than me. Clear days and starry nights continued to pass. Eventually I could make out sets of cliffs before me. I started to hear striking waves being shattered by jagged rocks as the surf came in. Finally I noticed a small beach within a sheltered cove as the cliffs began to diminish to the south.

My boat drifted onto the sand with the rolling waves; the sound of the fine glass crystals grating against my boat was an engaging symphony to my ears. I crawled out of the cockpit of the kayak, limping on the beach before collapsing. It was an odd feeling to be walking after spending so much time sitting on the surface of the water. I wept when I reached land. It began to rain. And the emotional journey that I had been on, nearly having been defeated by the foes of darkness, finally caught up with me. The fear, the anger, the loneliness that had been within my heart for so long needed to be released. Yet out there, somewhere, was a person who brought with them an experience of peace, rest, and hope. Tears streamed down my face, the last of the salt coming out of the ducts of my eyes, and the heavenly rain washing it away, cleansing me from everything I held on to. Fear, anger, and loneliness: all of it came to the surface, pouring out of me. It was a cool rain, but I did not worry about the anxiety of the grey skies that came with it.

It was not uncomfortable anymore. No, I began to feel refreshed. I began to feel clean. The grime was gone.

—

I found the girl, but I only felt emptiness. There were not even tears within me left to cry after my journey. The girl had said no; I know she did not say it, but she did not have to. I saw her, walking on the sidewalk, holding the hand of another man. She turned and looked at him, though she never saw me. She was smiling. And there, in the mystery of her eyes, was her peace. She had not battled wind, rain, and hunger in order to find what she was looking for. The tempest I had put myself through had not ultimately been worth it. But as I saw the joy in her eyes and the smile which was the true answer to the mystery of her being, I knew that I could not take it away from her. My suffering would be the cost of her peace; she would never know it. Dejected and depressed, I wondered if this was the final play of the gods of the ocean and the sky in their attempt to finally break my spirit. I imagined them now, a little bit beyond the horizon, laughing victoriously with each other, my spirit finally destroyed. This is what they had wanted the entire time, and now they had won. They had foreseen it all along; perhaps that was why they let me live, so that I could gain hope within my heart only to have it utterly crushed and stamped out.

She did not have the other half of my heart as I suspected she did; but as I watched her I soon began to realize that my emptiness was not a total vacuum like the space between planets and stars.

In the midst of the storm I had encountered hope, and yet despite seeing this girl walking hand-in-hand with someone else, that hope still lingered within me. I did not know why; reasonably speaking, I should have had no reason to live. I had poured my entire being into surviving this journey across an ocean for the purpose of being with her and she had denied that to me. She had given my heart back to me long ago; I had not realized it until now.

If it was not for this pestering spark of hope within me, I would have been as void as the desolate kayak that now sat on the beach; I could have wallowed in my miserable pity, sitting on the beach and staring to the setting sun in the west, ever so slowly becoming a shell of man. As far as I knew, I could have just sat there on the sand for the remainder of my days, slowly petrifying into a human shaped stone so that history could memorialize how foolish I was. Maybe if I became that rock, I would have been as eternal as the ocean and the sky, joining them as they waited for other souls to place bets on. If it was not for that persisting hope, life would have disappeared within me just as the light was disappearing from the horizon.

But it would not be so. As I looked out to the setting sun casting a beauty of gold, red, and purple I had never noticed before, a familiar yet still silhouetted figure appeared once again on the water before me. A voice spoke and the person held out their hand. "Follow me," said the voice.

That piece of hope, even though it may have been as small as one of those miniscule grains of glass sand that had run through my fingers earlier in the day, was not nearly as insignificant.

Somehow growing out of this hope, peace, encouragement, and purpose began to fill me once again. Before this figure, I knew the tempests and games of the ocean and sky would have no power over me. I stood up, grabbed the hand of this figure, and realized healing, restoration, and fullness.

Of Pigeons and Oilmen

Jim pushed through the double oak doors leading into the CEO's office. Bill, the company's old man, sat behind his mahogany desk; the computer, filled with company secrets, was positioned to the side. Bill did not want the machine to get in the way of face to face meetings. The steam was still rising from Bill's fresh mug of coffee; his secretary placed it on his desk almost as soon as the CEO arrived that morning. He leaned back in his leather chair, studying the morning paper and folding it into thirds as he examined the headlines. Behind Bill, just above his large office window, hung a small banner with the company's slogan: *Green Energy for a Green Country*.

Starla, Bill's secretary, stood by the door; her eyebrows were furrowed in helpless frustration due to Jim's intrusion. Bill looked up from his paper, first glancing at Jim, then noticing his annoyed secretary. He set the paper down next to his coffee.

"It's okay, Starla." The CEO smiled. "You can shut the door." Bill's words did not seem to make the secretary any happier. Even though she worked at NorthGreen Energy for close to five years, she never really liked Jim. Starla pulled the doors closed as she returned to her own desk. Bill picked up his coffee. Jim paced back and forth, holding the same central Pennsylvania paper in his own hands that Bill had already been reading. Bill took a sip from his mug, waiting for Jim to speak first.

Jim finally stood still. "Did you read today's paper?"

"I only got in the office maybe ten minutes before you, Jim.

I've just started reading the front page. Nothing really major seems to be going on." Bill paused for a moment. "You're the Vice President of Operations. Listen, I know you've got an important job, but you can't just barge into the CEO's office like this! Besides, we've got a meeting in 30 minutes to finalize the purchase of part of that refuge today. This couldn't wait?"

Jim appeared not to hear Bill's comment. "Page B2, Bill. Did you read it?" Bill looked at Jim, unsure of what to think of his employee. The CEO put down his coffee and opened the paper.

"Halfway down the page," Jim remarked.

"I see it, Jim. Thanks." Bill began reading the headline out loud. "Possible Passenger Pigeon Spotted." He skimmed the article. "Two birdwatchers at the New Kingdom Wildlife Refuge, located in the mountains of central Pennsylvania, believe they have recently seen the Passenger Pigeon, a once abundant bird thought to have gone extinct in 1914. One of the observers was carrying her camera and managed to snap a single picture before the bird flew away. The birdwatchers, a husband and wife, are extremely excited at the prospect of this discovery. Ornithologists and biologists from Penn State University, while skeptical, are not denying the idea of what they are calling 'a potential miracle from God.' Officials from the Department of Conservation and Natural Resources (DCNR), as well as officials from the Game Commission, will be in the area where the Passenger Pigeon was spotted over the next several weeks to months." Bill, usually in control of his emotions, started to clench his fist before taking a deep breath.

Jim spoke again. "You and I both know that there is a huge shale deposit underneath the New Kingdom Wildlife Refuge. We need a chunk of that land to get to the natural gas deposits down there."

"I know, Jim. You don't have to remind me." Bill's growing frustration was evident in his voice. He peered out the window behind his desk. "And to think we were on the verge of making a deal with them to purchase part of that refuge." He turned around. "Jim, to put it in energy terms, we're fracked."

"There's got to be some way to get that land, Bill. We don't even know if those hippies actually saw that dead bird or not," Jim began to rant. "That refuge shouldn't even be there! There are jobs at stake. There's energy at stake – energy that people need. We could be there today, ripping up trees, digging, drilling, and getting to that gas! Besides, we're NorthGreen Energy – *Green Energy for a Green Country* – right? When we're done in a few years, we'll plant a few trees, put up one or two big wind turbines for continued electricity, and no one will know the difference. No one will remember that stupid pigeon or that refuge. They'll see some grass field, a tree, and a windmill, and feel good that they bought energy from a company that's 'going green.'"

"Never mind that it would've been greener just to leave the poor land alone in the frst place," Bill pointed out, half sarcastically. "They're not going to sell us that land anymore, Jim. At least not today, tomorrow, or this year. If there really is an extinct bird there, the government won't even allow us near there. But give it a few years. People are addicted to energy. Forget that the majority of people who have ever lived on this earth have barely or never even used electricity, they think they need it today. Throw the word 'jobs' and 'economy' around, and we'll have public pressure mounting on that refuge and the government. People will be calling their representatives and senators. They'll fold eventually." Bill stopped for a moment before smirking. "And listen, I know that hydraulic fracturing is horrendous for the environment, but as long as we tell people we're a 'green' energy company, they'll believe it. The results for groundwater pollution and fracking were, let's just say, not good. Those studies will never see the light of day."

Despite his boss's attempt to joke about the situation, Jim did not find it funny. "If that passenger pigeon wasn't already extinct, it will be soon. It may have risen from the dead, but I'll make sure it returns to its grave."

Bill's desk phone buzzed. The CEO put it on speakerphone; it was Starla.

"Sir, Matt and Jean from the New Kingdom Wildlife Refuge are here."

"Thanks Starla. You can send them in." Bill turned to Jim. "Keep yourself together."

The CEO's office doors opened. The directors of the New Kingdom Wildlife Refuge came in. Bill smiled as he walked toward them. "Matt. Jean. Good to see you. I'm sure both of you are doing well this morning? I've heard the news about the pigeon; you must be excited!" Jim stood by the window, still unhappy.

"Thanks Bill. We are very excited at the refuge! Good to see you too," Jean replied.

"Let me introduce you to one of NorthGreen's vice presidents," Bill stated. Matt and Jean shook hands with Jim as he forced a smile. Bill gave Jim a displeased look. "Let's get down to business. Please have a seat." Bill returned to his leather chair. Matt and Jean sat down in two chairs in front of his desk.

Matt spoke up. "We've considered your offer, and while it is very tempting to sell a portion of the refuge to your company for that price, we've decided to hold onto it in light of the possible recent discovery."

Bill was not surprised. "I certainly understand. And I hope you reconsider. I think both of our organizations have common interests. The money you would make by selling that land would go a long way towards the preservation of the – what was the bird called again?"

"The Passenger Pigeon," Matt replied.

"Yes, the Passenger Pigeon. We strive to be as environmentally friendly as possible here, including the preservation of a thought-to-be-extinct bird!" Matt and Jean glanced at each other; there was something about NorthGreen Energy's CEO that they did not entirely trust.

"Well, we've made our decision. But thank you."

"If you change your mind, please let me know. You have my number." Matt and Jean got up as Bill walked them toward his office doors. "Enjoy the rest of your day."

Jim looked at Bill as he returned to his desk and logged on to his computer. "You're a smug son of a gun, Bill. You almost got those tree-huggers believing that you cared about that pigeon and their refuge."

"It's all part of the job, Jim. What's our slogan again?" Bill asked rhetorically. Jim glimpsed at the banner hanging above the window – *Green Energy for a Green Country*. "On your way out, tell Starla that we need to set up an appointment with the Vice President of Public Relations."

A Tale of Wisdom and Folly

Several years ago in a small rural town named Everyville there were two men named Alem and Terach. Both Alem and Terach were very fortunate because they had loving families. Each man had a beautiful wife, a son, and a daughter. They both lived in comparable houses, owned an equal amount of farmland, and raised the same number of livestock. For all intents and purposes, they were both two very similar people. In fact, there was really only one thing that separated them. Alem was humble and simply had a desire to take care of his family and provide for them honestly. On the other hand, Terach was prideful and always entertained the selfish thought of becoming rich and successful.

One day in the middle of a rainy summer a storm came along. The intense rains caused the river to flood. They both lost a portion of their farmland. The fierce winds caused the roofs on both of their barns to blow away. And finally, the large hail and loud thunder greatly distressed much of their livestock. They both wanted to recover from the storm damage so they could continue on with their lives.

It was well known that in the center of Everyville at the top of a hill lived an extremely old and wise woman who had more than double the years of farming experience of both Alem and Terach combined! Many people in the community went to her seeking advice and she helped all of them solve their problems. She freely gave out advice to those who earnestly sought after her wisdom.

Alem, who wanted to take care of his family and provide for

them in an honest manner went to the wise woman the day after this storm was over. He followed her advice exactly as she gave it because he knew she was so wise. Even when he had questions, he went back to her to find clarification. He learned more than he could have imagined from this woman and a year later, the number of his livestock increased, his fields were ready for farming again, and he had not only repaired his barn, but added on an addition for more equipment. He was able to show his deep love to his beautiful wife, son, and daughter by providing for them. Alem was a very happy person.

Unfortunately, Terach was foolish and deliberated whether he should see the wise woman. He wondered if he should just try to fix everything by himself. Finally, after a month of being frustrated, he went to the center of town to see her. However, just outside her home there was another very beautiful young woman walking on the street. Terach noticed her and went over to talk to her before he ever got the chance to see the wise woman. Enthralled by her young beauty, she told him that she would not only be able to fix everything on his farm, but also double the amount of his land and livestock if Terach gave her some of his money. She even promised him a barn three times the size of his current one so that he could store all of his new farm equipment. Terach's heart was taken captive by the thought of so much success.

A year later, Terach had not solved any of his problems. His land was still in complete disarray and the majority of his livestock were either sick or dead. Every month, the young woman took more and more of his money; he could no longer feed his family or his livestock. He could not take care of his farmland. His beautiful wife had taken his son and daughter away because Terach could no longer provide for them. He only saw death and despair around him at his once beautiful home.

Finally, the young woman invited Terach to her home one day. She gave him instructions on how to get there from the center of town. When he had finally arrived, he realized that it was his own farm. She now owned his land and lived on it. The young beautiful woman who had promised so much had only delivered barren farmland, dead animals, and a broken family.

In one last attempt to do something right, he went and saw the wise old woman. She smiled and asked him why he had not come to her immediately after the storm. He had no answer for her. She gave a small chuckle and told him that she could no longer help him. She said to Terach: "I have been around a long time and have seen everything. There are consequences for your actions and it is time to accept them. Your friend Alem came to me and continually asked for my advice over the past year. Why did not you do the same? I would have freely given it to you.

"A long time ago I wrote, 'Since they would not accept my advice and spurned my rebuke, they will eat the fruit of their ways and be filled with the fruit of their schemes. For the waywardness of the simple will kill them, and the complacency of fools will destroy them; but whoever listens to me will live in safety and be at ease, without fear of harm.' The same is true today, Terach."

Babble, Part Three

"Oph." The voice was quiet and distant.

I opened my eyes, blinking several times. Despite my blurry vision, I recognized the shapes of trees growing into a blue sky above me. Stiff blades of grass poked into the feathers on my back. Clarity was slowly conquering the haziness of my sleep. There was light and warmth, but it did not come from the sun above. It almost seemed to emanate from the voice itself, that although quiet and distant, was awakening me.

"Oph." The voice was familiar.

I knew this voice. I had heard it before, but I could not recall exactly where. It had been a part of my life once, perhaps in the background of my subconscious. Maybe it had always simply been a given in my sustainment, and I was just now discerning that truth. It was a voice that, as I pondered over it more, drew life into it, but at the same time gave life from it. There was both strength and peace in this voice. They were the strength and peace of a memory that was returning to my mind.

"Oph." The voice was clear.

It grew stronger as its power resonated throughout my body. This voice was not only talking to me, but speaking life itself into me. The recollection of Mrs. Nachosh's words echoed in my ears: "A more accurate name might be 'The In Dweller.'" Her musings were correct. I remembered more of Mrs. Nachosh's words: "You've known love your whole life, given to you by your family, friends, and by 'The High – or rather – In – Dweller' him-ss-self."

It was the same voice that spoke to the two humans walking in the garden; it was 'The High Dweller' who was calling my name. But Mrs. Nachosh mentioned something else after she spoke of the love of 'The High Dweller'; I knew it was important, but I could not readily recall what she said.

The voice did not speak my name a fourth time. A figure was standing above me, shaped like one of the two humans from the garden. My vision, although steadily becoming clearer, was still fuzzy enough that I could only recognize that it was a man. I couldn't yet see his details. He reached down, carefully put his hands around my wings as he picked me up off of my back, and lifted me into the air. My head ached for only a moment before the dull pain disappeared completely.

The man placed his hand gently upon my head. My vision returned to the perfect eyesight I had known my entire life. I could see the distinct outlines of rustling green leaves on the trees around me, the rough patterns of bark on their trunks, and the sharpness of individual blades of vibrant grass below them.

The man removed his hand from my head and straightened his arm. As he allowed me to perch myself on his forearm, I noticed distinct markings on each of his wrists that the two humans from the garden never had. I extended my wings; it was good to fully stretch them. They felt cramped, as if I had been asleep in the same position for an extremely long time. I took a deep breath and filled my lungs with crisp, fresh air.

"Oph." I repeated my name to myself. It was who I am. It was the perfect name, given to me by the two humans in the garden. In every way, I was the bird I was created to be.

I turned my gaze from the trees and the grass, back to the man's wrists, and then finally to his face. I did not see the likeness of either of the two humans from the garden, but someone else. It was someone who, although I had never seen his face before, was very familiar.

"Oph, do you know who I am?" His voice was clear; in it was peace, yet also strength. It was a voice of great power, yet a voice of considerable joy, contentment, and fulfillment. It was a voice of the love that Mrs. Nachosh had described.

"I know your voice," I replied. "But I do not know your face." The man smiled.

"Of course you know my voice." The man paused, a deeper smile on his face. "I was there at your birth and throughout your life. I was there at the births and throughout the lives of your parents and their parents before them. I was there at the births and throughout the lives of all of your friends' parents. And for each of your descendents after you, I was there at all of their births and throughout their lives." The man continued to look at me as he spoke. "I was there since before the dawn of the age that you lived in; in fact, I created that age, I redeemed the next age, and I remade it in this age. I have been, I am, and I always will be. You have known my voice; you have known my Spirit." As I remained standing on his arm, the man's eyes searched me, examining me, knowing me, and piercing into my very being. "Mrs. Nachosh was right to say that I am 'The In Dweller.' My Spirit has sustained your life; my Spirit sustains all life. Apart from me, there is no life." He paused again. "And now, Oph, you know my face."

In the presence of 'The High – or rather – In – Dweller' himself, joy, contentment, peace, and fulfillment poured through my body. Love, emanating from this man in front of me, embraced my heart, body, and mind. Performing the only appropriate response I could even consider, I brought my wings into my body and bowed my head before the face of this human above all other humans, 'The High Dweller' himself. He brought his arm back toward him and placed his hand upon my head one more time. The man, this one like the other two humans I had seen before, kneeled down and set me on the ground before him.

"May I ask you a question?" I asked.

"Certainly. Ask anything you like."

"My head – why did it ache for a moment when you picked me up, then go away?"

He stood back up. "You would not recognize it, Oph; you lived in an age before its complete effects could be seen. Death entered the world. It is what you experienced when you fell from the tree. Your friends, the two humans whom I loved very much, separated themselves from me. And because they separated themselves from me, life separated itself from them. Death resulted. Like a disease, it destroyed, ravaged, and consumed the paradise that I created to function in the harmony of my love.

"There was one who accused me and was intent on my failure; he overtook one of my creatures, your friend Mr. Nachosh, who then convinced the humans to disobey me, thus separating themselves from the sustaining life of my eternal spirit. In me, there is life; there is love. And in my love, there is life. Apart from me, there is no life; there is no love. And without my love, there is no life.

"An entire age, broken in death, and broken as my creation distanced themselves from the life of my eternal Spirit, has passed since that moment when death first began its infection across my world; but since then, I began remaking that creation into something new, repairing it, and utilizing those of my creation who desired to return to me. There were two realities, intertwined, as I wove them toward one reality of resurrection and life. My realm of eternity broke into the realm of death. And now it has been remade; I have completely destroyed death and all of its effects forever. The one who accused me and was intent on my failure – he is gone."

"Oh." I looked toward the ground; I did not entirely understand what 'The High Dweller' was explaining, but he was also speaking about things that I had evidently only partly experienced when I fell from the tree. But it didn't matter; I did not need to understand completely. I had faith in 'The High Dweller,' and I knew that was all that really mattered. "So is that one of the reasons why my wings felt cramped?"

'The High Dweller' chuckled lightheartedly.

"You have been asleep for a very long time, Oph." He smiled again as he looked at me.

"Oh." I thought again. "Well that makes a lot more sense!"

"It certainly does!" 'The High Dweller' laughed once more.

It was very thoughtful of him to spend this much time talking with me; he is a very patient man. One would think that for a person who did so much important work and had so much power, he would always be away doing something great. Nonetheless, something told me that he was doing the exact work he wanted to do at that very moment. I could not help but smile.

Suddenly, as I stood by 'The High Dweller,' the rest of Mrs. Nachosh's words returned to my memory: "But now it has grown into a greater love!" I remembered who was next to me when I fell from the tree!

"Yaphah!" I exclaimed.

'The High Dweller' kneeled down next to me once again.

"Oph, do you trust me?" he asked.

I did not hesitate to answer. "Yes! How could I not trust you?"

"Good. Then follow me. We will take a walk. But of course, Oph, you may fly if you like! It will be good for you to exercise your wings after you have been asleep for so long." 'The High Dweller' winked at me. "There is someone whom I would like you to meet."

"Is it Yaphah?" I asked excitedly. My heart beat quickly when I said her name.

"It is another human, but that is all I will say for now. I know that you trust me, Oph." I did not doubt 'The High Dweller.'

I extended my wings again, flapped them once, and lifted myself off the ground. It was good to fly. I flapped them several more times and rose through the air; strength and energy pulsed through my body as the air passed over my feathers. I flew higher, stretched my wings, and soared.

Among all sorts of creatures that I had never seen before, I saw a grey wolf lying next to a small lamb, watching over it. A leopard, always vigilant, stood next to a goat munching on the green grass. A calf, a beautiful lion, and a newborn deer, walked together behind what appeared to be the child of a human. The lion stopped for a moment to eat the grass below it. There was a mother cow and a mother bear, both keeping an eye on their calves and their cubs as they played with one another in the shade of the trees. There were several more humans with their children, gathered together and listening attentively to a snake telling, as Mrs. Nachosh would say, its ssssss-serpentine tale.

I flapped my wings and dropped back towards the earth, gliding closer to 'The High Dweller.'

"Nothing looks different from the world that you once knew, Oph. And all is at it should be," 'The High Dweller' said. "Except, I suppose, there are a lot more humans and creatures than were in existence when I first created you!"

"You have made a beautiful world," I replied.

"Many of these humans never knew the garden that you grew up in, Oph. The bear cub playing joyfully with the calf, the lion walking peacefully with the lamb, the cat being good friends with the mouse – these are new things for many of the humans. But to you, it is the same as it was; but many did not know the age that you knew. You would not believe it, Oph, but during the age of death, many of my animal creatures did not even know who or what they were." 'The High Dweller' paused once more and breathed in the air of his creation. "But all is set right." He turned to look at me as I flew next to him. "It truly is a beautiful world. It truly is good. It is as I intended it to be."

"May I ask you one more question?" I stated.

"You are a curious bird, Oph. But I created your kind to be that way. What is your question?"

"My friends, Mr. and Mrs. Nachosh, and Akbar and Tsiyyi, will I see them again?"

"I have not forgotten a single one of my creatures; you will see Mr. and Mrs. Nachosh, and Akbar and Tsiyyi, again. But you must be patient; there is something I must ask you to do first."

I looked ahead. There was a young woman; she had a face like the one whom all the other creatures I knew called 'Life.' She had long dark hair and bright eyes; as I looked at her, I saw that her existence was true to the name of the first woman. She smiled widely when she saw 'The High Dweller' approaching, revealing the love that was the core of her life. I flapped my wings once again and landed next to her. She turned and looked at me. There was peace, joy, contentment, and fulfillment when I looked at her face.

"Prisca," 'The High Dweller' spoke.

The woman kneeled down before him. "My King."

"My good and faithful servant, rise." The woman stood up before 'The High Dweller,' her eyes shining in the presence of the creator who she called her King.

"Prisca, I would like you to meet my friend Oph." 'The High

Dweller' turned his head toward me. "Oph, I would like you to meet my friend Prisca."

I extended my wing and held it out toward her as she touched it with her hand.

"Prisca and Oph, there is some work that is calling me elsewhere. I must go tend to it, but I would like to meet you at the gates to the city of my Father." 'The High Dweller' raised his hand and pointed to the east. "It will not take you long to reach it. As you journey, talk with one another." His voice of strength, clarity, and peace reassured me.

I folded my wings into my body and bowed my head. Prisca, once more, kneeled down. In the presence of the loving creator, one's only desire was to show reverence. A moment later, I lifted my head; he had disappeared. I took a deep breath and smiled as Prisca stood back up.

We turned east and began our walk together. On the horizon, I could see the outline of a city upon a hill. We were still several miles away, though even in the daylight the city glowed. It was as if its walls were constructed of a bright gold, illuminating a central light into the world.

A river flowed from the hill. Its rushing blue water cut through the lush green landscape. Fish leaped from the river; lions and sheep, bears and deer, and humans and all sorts of other creatures lined its banks, drinking from its fresh water.

Prisca spoke. "Is there someone you are looking for, Oph?" My heart beat faster as I thought of Yaphah.

"Her name is Yaphah. She is the most beautiful bird that has ever existed." I paused as I thought of her. "Her eyes are breathtaking. The red feathers on her tail are stunning. Every time I even think of Yaphah, my heart pounds like I've been racing through the sky all day and I can barely catch my breath!"

"I know how you feel, Oph. There is a man who I felt the same way about."

"Who is he?" I asked.

"His name is Aquila. We grew up together and we were born just days apart from each other. Our parents named us after two of the people that Paul wrote about in scripture."

I was curious. "Who is Paul and what is scripture?"

"Scripture is the story of how the King – or as I've learned, many of the animals just call him 'The High Dweller' – redeemed the world. Paul is one of the people from that story!"

"Paul is a human then?"

"Yes!" She returned to her story as we walked. "But Aquila and I were born in Constantinople, the great capital city of the Byzantines." She must have seen that I was still confused. "I'll do my best to explain."

"It's okay. Hawks are very simple thinkers."

"Nonetheless, Oph, you are still a very smart bird! The smartest one I've met. But...." She waited a moment before finishing. "You are the only bird here whom I've met!"

We laughed together. "I'll do my best to follow along. What happened to Aquila?"

Prisca stopped walking. "We fell in love with each other. Like you said, Oph, when I saw him, my heart beat faster. And I knew that when he saw me, his heart beat faster. We were happy together. We both wanted to spend the rest of our lives together. We decided to marry each other." She turned her eyes toward the ground. "We often walked to a field just outside the walls of the city. There were small purple flowers that grew there. Each time we went, Aquila always picked the most beautiful flower he could find in that field and gave it to me before we returned to the city. It was a symbol of the love we had for each other." I remembered the flower and the small bundle of twigs I had found to give to Yaphah.

"We were going to be married in the Hagia Sophia, the beautiful church of Holy Wisdom in Constantinople. But in the days before our ceremony, the Westerners started their siege of our city on their way to one of their crusades. Aquila and I, together with our families, hid in our home for days. One afternoon, Aquila decided to go the church to join others in prayer for the safety of our city. A few hours later, I decided to go as well. I did not want to be apart from him."

Prisca looked directly at me. "I could never forget that day, Oph. It was April 13, 1204, in the year of our Lord. Aquila had just walked out of the church. I was about to run to meet him when I saw one of the crusaders approach him. He had a sword in his hand. They had been stealing treasures from all over the city, and finally came to the Hagia Sophia for its relics. I could not hear what Aquila and the Westerner said to each other, but the man with the sword began to yell at Aquila. The crusader tried to walk past Aquila toward the church. Aquila stepped in front of him." Prisca began to walk towards the city again. We were close. Its walls were decorated with radiant stones. There were multiple gates with white doors, all of them open.

"I was so scared, Oph." She took another breath. "The man picked up his sword and drove it into Aquila's chest. Then he pushed Aquila to the side, walked past him, and entered the church. I ran to Aquila. I held him as he bled. I told him that I loved him. I cried. But I also told him that it was not the end; I told him that we would see one another again.

"I didn't know what to do. I just ran back to the house, hid, and mourned. Months later, I went back to the field of flowers just outside the city walls. I returned there often; each time I went, I picked a flower for myself. I knew the day would come when I would see Aquila once more. I knew that we would be together, forever. I knew that the King would set things right."

I looked up at Prisca. Her eyes were bright and full of hope. "And the King has set things right, Oph."

I held out my wing toward her and touched her hand. "I had just given Yaphah a gift – a flower and leafy twigs; birds like twigs. We were about to fly with each other over the garden as the sun was setting. And that is when this thing called death happened." I paused and looked into Prisca's eyes. "We can trust 'The High Dweller.' We can trust the King. You will see Aquila again and I will see Yaphah again."

"I know." Prisca smiled.

By now we were just outside the city's golden walls. Prisca took a sudden breath at its beauty. "It is just like it had been described – golden walls, jasper and sapphire, agate and emerald, onyx and carnelian and ruby, chrysolite and beryl, topaz and turquoise, jacinth and amethyst, and the twelve gates inlaid with the purest pearl." A light, shining with the most intense brightness I had ever seen, was coming from inside the city. It was inviting, drawing us closer to it, and there was warmth in it.

"Look, Prisca, over there!" I stretched out my wing. "There is 'The High Dweller,' and he is with a man and a bird! It must be Aquila and Yaphah!" Prisca began running toward them. I flapped my wings and began to fly. My heart was pounding!

I looked toward 'The High Dweller.' His robes were white, shimmering in the midst of the light from the city. He wore a sash across his chest, golden like the city's walls. His warm eyes radiated his love with the energy of a roaring fire. His hair was white, his feet were like bronze, and his face was gleaming like the sun.

"Welcome to the Holy City of my Father. My Spirit is its warmth. I am its light." His voice resonated with the strength of the river flowing out from the city, while at the same time cutting through the air with precision and power. As he looked toward us, there was nothing in my heart except the singular overwhelming force of joy, peace, contentment, and fulfillment. It was the true experience of the great love and life of 'The High Dweller.'

He smiled deeply. I looked at Yaphah; she was even more beautiful than when I fell asleep to death so long ago. 'The High Dweller' spoke again. "Oph and Prisca. I have asked Yaphah and Aquila to gather something very important on their way to the gates of the Holy City of my Father."

He turned to Yaphah. In her beak, she held a flower, fully grown, its petals purple, vibrant, and glowing with life. Aquila produced the same flower in his hand.

"Prisca and Aquila. You have been faithful. You have endured. I love you both, and you have both loved me," the King stated. Aquila gave Prisca the flower just as he had done so many times before, yet this time the flower, now eternal, would not face the pain of death.

"Yaphah and Oph. You, as well, are my beautiful creation."

Yaphah stepped toward me.

'The High Dweller' kneeled down and smiled at both of us. "Yaphah, may I hold this for you while you speak?" She dropped the eternal flower in 'The High Dweller's open hand.

Yaphah gazed into my eyes. "Do you want to fly together?" I looked toward 'The High Dweller' as he stood back up, holding the flower in his hand, then looked back toward Yaphah.

Yaphah and I smiled at each other as we both flapped our wings, almost effortlessly, and lifted ourselves off the ground in front of the magnificent city of 'The High Dweller.' As we climbed through the air, we looked below us, watching 'The High Dweller' turn and walk through the shining gates. Prisca and Aquila grabbed one another's hands as they followed their King into the golden city.

Yaphah and I spread our wings as we soared above the city, scanning the new earth and all the amazing life that existed upon it.

Yaphah looked at me and grinned. She touched the edge of her wing with the edge of mine.

"You know, Oph," she said. "It seems like 'The High Dweller' is not even half the description!"

"I think you're right, Yaphah." There was truly no description that would ever entirely fit the complete love, life, and power of the man whom Prisca and Aquila followed into the golden city. I turned my gaze back to the earth below me. In the distance I saw my friends. Akbar the mouse and Tsiyyi the cat were playing, and Mr. and Mrs. Nachosh were talking to each other, probably telling their ssss-serpentine tales.

Like 'The High – or rather – In – Dweller' said, "All is set right." It is as he intended it to be, beautiful and good.

Appendices:

Scripture References	123
Reflections on the Writing Process	125
On Love	131

Scripture References

Babble, Part One: Genesis 1-3

Seven Days: Genesis 8:6-12

The Defeat of the Amorites: Joshua 10:1-27

After Death: 1 Samuel 28:14-16

Antietam: 1 Kings 12:24

1 Kings 12: 1 Kings 12:25-33

The Fall of Belshazzar: Daniel 5

The Ammonite Messenger: Nehemiah 2:1-10

Luke 9:23: Luke 9:23

Babble, Part Two: Mark 15:33-41; 16:1-8; Matthew 27:45-56; 28:1-10; Luke 23:44-49; 24:1-12; John 19:28-30; 20:1-10

Across an Ocean: Mark 6:47-52

Of Pigeons and Oilmen: Nehemiah 2

A Tale of Wisdom and Folly: Proverbs 1-9

Babble, Part Three: Isaiah 11; John 1:1-18; Revelation 1:12-16; 21; 22

*All quoted scripture references are from the New Revised Standard Version.

Reflections on the Writing Process

Recently I had the opportunity to develop various aspects of my creative writing through a directed study at Nazarene Theological Seminary with the Assistant Dean, Dr. Keith Schwanz. It was a great experience and provided valuable feedback in developing my writing. Several of the stories in this anthology are a result of this class.

The simple activity of doing creative writing assignments on a regular basis was by far the most beneficial for improvement (really, this is not that profound of a statement at all)! As with any activity, the best way to get better is to practice; the same is true for writing. As I read, re-read, and edited, I looked carefully at each individual word, sentence, and paragraph; I not only asked myself if these were the words that I wanted to say, but also if the structure was how I wanted to express them. Although ultimately word choice, structure, and rhythm (sometimes I call the flow of the writing 'rhythm') could be considered elements of an individual writer's style.

Again, and more than anything else, sitting down and writing a few thousand words each week has done the most to improve my writing. As I stated earlier, it could almost be considered practice. The more an individual writes, whether it is for creative purposes or non-creative purposes (but hopefully all writing has a creative element to it), the more an individual will be able to clearly articulate what he or she is thinking; they will be better able to form words into a coherent story or essay. Granted, each time someone writes, they will probably not produce something worth publishing (sometimes not even worth reading); some days a person may sit down and all that comes out is dribble. Nevertheless, this is still an important part of the process! There are some days when I just have to spill out the thoughts in my mind, even if it is in an extremely inelegant fashion. In the past, I have termed this (oftentimes painful) process a "brain-dump." I literally just try to dump out whatever is floating around in my mind onto a piece of paper; the result is usually not pretty. I must remember that I can come back at a later date and do a lot of necessary editing; I can then shape and form those initial ideas into more clearly thought out concepts. Rough drafts can be extremely rough - but that is okay; that is why they are called rough drafts.

The initial brainstorming process, while critical, can be fun! It goes without saying that additional brainstorming also occurs during the actual writing; as someone writes, new ideas are born (some are good; some are bad), and the writer makes any necessary changes to improve the story. In my writing assignments from this semester, when I had to retell a biblical story and then revamp it to share the scripture from a different or modern setting, I had a certain process to come up with ideas. Typically, I would read the chapter from scripture, i.e. Joshua 10, etc., and then simply let the passage sit in my mind for a day or two. If there was any certain part of the passage that seemed more intriguing, I might focus on those verses more. I would also try to discern what the overall point of the verses were, and how they fit into the overarching story of the Bible. I would then take all of these ideas - the whole chapter, intriguing or unique aspects of the chapter, and the overarching ideas of the Bible - and throw them into the cooking pot that is my mind. I let them simmer in there for a while. Asking questions about perspective, point-of-view, plot, characters, historical events, modern day events, etc., often helps cook these ideas into a story concept that that is both original and creative. While I used this process with scripture in order to tell a "new" story about it, it can also be used with any other ideas that a writer has. Take the ideas in your mind, let them simmer, mix them up, and see what happens! Have fun with it. Let your imagination go wild with possibilities.

Sometimes this process might take a couple days; sometimes it might take a week or a couple weeks. Sometimes ideas might be simmering for months or years. However, one must still realize that this is not a mathematical formula that will guarantee amazing ideas; the good ideas might actually be more rare. Having the patience to refine ideas into something a writer can work with is essential.

It may still even be necessary to perform a "brain-dump." The "brain-dump," (though it might not be pleasant) forces the writer to get his or her ideas on paper. They may come back to it later, find an idea that they like in it, combine some new concept that they thought of later, and then edit and transform what they may have once considered dribble into a good story that is both original and creative. Plus, it helps a writer "practice." There are good days and bad days of practice; bad days, it seems, are inevitable. But the more one practices, the more likely that the good days will increasingly outnumber the bad days.

Once you get what you want to say written down, then you must look at how you want to say it. Even if the writer has to spill out the "what" of the words onto paper, it is still a good idea to go back and look at the "how" that you are saying them. Think of the scene that you are trying to set. Consider the emotions and reactions you want people to feel. Reflect on the rhythm and style of the story; look at varying the sentence and paragraph structures so that it will keep the story moving in a way that flows easily for reading. In a novel or short story, one doesn't always want to read the same scene description that might be found in a play or movie script. Movies have visual scenes to make the story come alive and progress it forward; the writer has words. Review what imagery you can use to make the story flow forward in your style. Look at each individual part of the sentence - the adjectives, verbs, adverbs (but don't get very heavy on the adverbs), nouns, etc. Ask yourself if you are sure that those words are the words that best describe what you are trying to convey. Ask yourself if there is a better way to convey the thought, emotion, setting, individual, etc. Use a thesaurus! Every time I write, I have a thesaurus open on my desktop; it not only helps me use variety, but it often helps me find a better word that I did not originally think of.

Once the writer has made it this far into the editing stage, it is a good idea to set it aside and focus on something else for an hour or two, or a day or two. Sometimes it might simply be taking a walk outside to clear your mind. Then come back to the story and ask yourself the same editing questions again (Is this exactly how I want to convey this thought? Etc.). Let your friends and family look at it and allow them to give you their thoughts. Be confident in your writing so that you don't take criticisms personally, but also be willing to recognize the validity of any changes or ideas that they suggest! They may see something that you missed. They will often ask questions to help you further refine your story into something even better.

This directed study has been a great experience in creative writing. It has challenged me to examine and refine the way I write; though I am sure that my writing will continue to be refined for as long as I am alive! I am not sure that anyone quite "arrives," but just continues to improve. Developing the story into something better through editing, word choice, and sentence and paragraph structures, comes with time. Most importantly though, it starts with the simple act of writing. Whether the words comes out in an elegant fashion after simmering and cooking in your mind, or whether they fall out in an chaotic and unorganized "brain-dump," the activity of writing is by far the best way to improve writing, for whatever purposes one wants to write!

On Love

John 15:9-17 (NRSV)

9 As the Father has loved me, so I have loved you; abide in my love.
10 If you keep my commandments, you will abide in my love, just as I have kept my Father's commandments and abide in his love.
11 I have said these things to you so that my joy may be in you, and that your joy may be complete.
12 "This is my commandment, that you love one another as I have loved you.
13 No one has greater love than this, to lay down one's life for one's friends.
14 You are my friends if you do what I command you.
15 I do not call you servants any longer, because the servant does not know what the master is doing; but I have called you friends, because I have made known to you everything that I have heard from my Father.
16 You did not choose me but I chose you. And I appointed you to go and bear fruit, fruit that will last, so that the Father will give you whatever you ask him in my name.
17 I am giving you these commands so that you may love one another.

At the core of this passage is Jesus' instruction for his followers to love one another. These are instructions that are demonstrated by Christ's life and teachings; it is also a theme that is present in both the Old and New Testaments. In fact, mostly everyone knows the latter half of 1 John 4:8; we recite it to each other all the time: "God is love." However, many times in talking about love, whether it be the love of Christ or the love of God, or even in our culture when popular or well-respected authority figures instruct us just to "love one another," we never really elaborate on what defines love. One of the most popular songs by the "Black-Eyed Peas" is titled "*Where is the love?*" Another song from the early 1990s by (the musical "great") Haddaway asks, "*What is love?*" Movies, popular music, books, poetry, and philosophy: they all talk about love. Most of the time (though not all of the time), answers about love are not very deep and only skim the surface.

We rarely hear a description of what love actually is. Maybe it is simply assumed that we know? Or maybe we just think we know? A lot of what we think we know is actually just about the feeling or emotion of love itself. But as many of us know, feelings of love come and go; feelings are fleeting. Even if love feels so strong, that feeling still may dissipate after years and years. And if we, humanity, really think that we have got a grip or a handle on what love really is, why is it that everyday on the news we hear about wars in various parts of the world, someone being shot on the street corner, a store being robbed downtown, a millionaire banker stealing millions more in their greed, or pop culture stars (ironically, they are often times the very same ones who are telling us that all we need to do is "love one another") getting divorced and married to someone else after only a couple months? Not only does so much of humanity base its idea of love off of only a feeling or an emotion, but how are we supposed to know what love is, if on a daily basis humanity is separating itself from God – God, who is the very beginning of all love, the author of all love, and where all love flows from and out of?

Humanity separates itself from God through our very own sinfulness and selfishness; but true to what love actually is and not what we think love is, and true to God's eternal demonstration of that love, God still shows us and demonstrates his love to us whether it is through grace, patience, mercy, protection, justice, and blessing and granting our needs and prayers. God does not base love, his holy love, off of only a fleeting feeling or emotion, but through a practice of love. And it is a practice of love that is found in sacrifice and obedience to God which we can build our love with. Perhaps today, each one of us must change our concept of love from feelings and emotions to a practice of love that is consistent with the practice of love that God continually demonstrates to each one of us. Perhaps our view of love needs to be reoriented so that it does not have a foundation in us, but rather that it becomes a love that has a foundation in God; then we may truly find what love actually is and learn how to show that love to one another.

What, exactly, is this love? Christ tells us in verse 12: "This is my commandment, that you love one another as I have loved you." Christ tells us in verse 17: "I am giving you these commands that you may love one another." But Christ does not stop there; Christ elaborates on what exactly his love is. It is not a fleeting feeling or emotion that comes and goes, but it is a practice of love that finds eternal fulfillment; it is a love that gives us joy, it is a love that gives Christ himself joy, and it is a love that gives others joy.

Love means sacrifice. Christ says: "This is my commandment, that you love one another as I have loved you." He then follows this piece of instruction with: "No one has greater love than this, to lay down one's life for one's friends." Christ is, in fact, alluding to his very own death, saying that his death is an act of love for his friends. His own death is a sacrifice of himself so that humanity, and you and I, might be reconciled to God. But Christ tells us to "love one another as I have loved you." Christ loved us so much that he was willing to die for us so that ultimately we may be together with him. Sacrifice to the point of death: that is the depth of love that Christ has for us, yet it is also the depth of love that Christ desires us to have for other people. Sacrifice is an integral part of love for others; we, as followers and friends of Christ, are called to that level of love for one another. Perhaps today it may not mean death; but what does it mean? Our lives are valuable to us, but what else is valuable to us? Time? Money? Material goods? Food? Water? Shelter? Our unique skills? Perhaps this level of love means sacrificing those things for others when they are in need so that we may show the love of Christ to our neighbors. Perhaps it means a death of our selfish selves, and living anew in Christ, so that we may freely give of these things in a way that is like the love of Christ. (We cannot forget that there are countless numbers of people living in poverty all over the world. Many of them are Christians; our own brothers and sisters are going without food, clean water, and shelter everyday. What does loving them through sacrifice look like in your life?)

Love means obeying God. Christ foreshadows that love is "to lay down one's life for one's friends," but then adds the stipulation: "You are my friends *if* you do what I command you." Christ also tells his disciples in verse 10: "*If* you keep my commandments, you will abide in my love, just as I have kept my Father's commandments and abide in his love." Here is Christ's commandment: "That you love one another as I have loved you." Christ calls on us to live in obedience to God and to Christ. It is an exercise in the selfless nature, not the selfish nature, to live in obedience to another. Christ even calls those who live in keeping with the commandments his friends. Perhaps in our own lives, living selflessly and not selfishly, to others is what the practice of love actually is. Maybe this means taking the time to listen to another's story. Maybe this means giving of yourself in a way where there is no gain for you. Maybe it means spending time with another person who you do not necessarily want to spend time with. Maybe it means humility and respecting another person's wishes. Sacrifice and selflessness: these are examples of what love actually is. Both of these are demonstrated by Christ.

God loves all of us; in fact, there is so much love within God that in the beginning, God created people. From the very beginning, and from the outpouring of God's love, God desired to be in relation with others; that is the reason God created us – so that we may be in communion with God and with each other. In fact, it is something that is evident in the very nature and character of God himself! If we look at God, God is one, but God is also three (in one); three very distinct aspects of God all in relation with one another in the trinity – God is relational even within himself. And God is love; out of this relational and self-giving love, God created humanity. God created the world that we live in. God created the mountains, the oceans, the atmosphere, and the land that we walk on. God created the birds, the deer that roam the woods, the big cats of the jungle, the fish that populate the sea, the bees that pollinate the vividly colored flowers in our gardens, and even the snakes that slither around, all to be in harmony and balance with one another. And out of love, God entrusted us to have a role in taking care of this world. (The responsibility we have as stewards of God's creation is something that we simply cannot forget about, but it is critical as we give others a glimpse into the kingdom of God. Out of love for God, love for others, and love for what God has made, we must therefore do a better job of fulfilling this responsibility.)

And out of love God gave us free will, even if that meant the possibility of turning against the very one who created us, even if that meant that people may choose to live in disobedience to God and even if that meant the resulting physical manifestations of evil, sickness, and disease within this world, things that have come about from living in a world filled with generations of people who have long since removed themselves from a foundation of love in God.

But it also means, by the basic characteristic of freedom found in love, we may choose to respond to God's grace and the love that is inherent in his kingdom. It is only in the hope we have in Christ and the renewing of ourselves by the Holy Spirit, and by the present work we are called to in the kingdom of God in this world, that these evils will be overcome.

Nevertheless, out of love and desire for God to be in communion with us and for us to be in communion with God, God loved humanity even in our sinfulness against him. God chose a group of people as his own, and through that group of people, all the people of the world would one day be reconciled to him. God made a covenant with Abraham that his offspring would be as numerous as the stars. And through Israel, and through Christ, through whom we Gentiles are grafted in to God's chosen people of Israel, becoming one of God's chosen people in the Church today, that covenant and promise with Abraham still holds true. It is through Christ and the Church today that God calls us to live out his message of practicing love in both sacrifice and selflessness.

Moreover, as a testament to God's grace and love, God provided a way for humanity to return to him through both obedience and faith in God. In the Old Testament, this was the law given to Moses; that through this law, the Israelites in their own disobedience to God, might be once again reconciled to God. Part of that involved sacrifice in order to atone for their sins, a sacrifice of their very best animals and livestock to God. God desired their best; today God desires the very best of what we have to offer. However, today this is not through the sacrifice of animals and livestock, but in our time, our talents, our skills, our belongings, and in fact, you and me. God asks us to give it all over to him and God asks us to give ourselves over to him in obedience.

In the Old Testament, ultimately it was a law that taught love.

The prophet Micah tells us the meaning of the law, writing: "He has told you, O mortal, what is good; and what does the Lord require of you but to do justice, and to love kindness, and to walk humbly with your God?" (Micah 6:8). In Mark, when a scribe asks Christ what the most important commandment is, Christ tells him: "The first is, 'Hear, O Israel: the Lord our God, the Lord is one; you shall love the Lord your God with all your heart, and with all your soul, and with all your mind, and with all your strength.' The second is this, 'You shall love your neighbor as yourself.' There is no other commandment greater than these" (Mark 12:29-31). Paul, an expert in the Jewish law, tells the Church in Galatia: "For the whole law is summed up in a single commandment, "You shall love your neighbor as yourself" (Galatians 5:14). And here, in this passage in John, Christ tells us: "This is my commandment, that you love one another as I have loved you." The meaning of the law: to love God with everything that we are and to love each other in the same way that God loves us and in the same way that we love God. This is a practice of love that involves sacrifice and selflessness.

Ultimately, as Israel abused this law and its rulers and religious leaders manipulated and exploited this law and obedience to God, God sent his own son, Jesus Christ, so that the law of love in obedience to God may be made known: Jesus Christ, who was there from the very beginning, who is part of the trinitarian, relational, loving nature of God, and who is love itself. In this way, Jesus Christ is the manifestation of the law given to Israel; Jesus Christ is the fulfillment of that law. The law given to Israel was meant for love; Christ, the manifestation and fulfillment of the law, is love itself.

However, just as Christ tells us in this passage that "No one has greater love than this, to lay down one's life for one's friends," Christ alludes to and foreshadows his very own death. The law demanded sacrifice of the very best, and in order for Christ to truly fulfill this law it meant his own death. This moment, of Christ suffering and dying on a cross which was designed for humiliation and shame, is God's love embodied in a practice of sacrifice and selflessness. However, in this atoning death of Christ, it not only meant a redemption for the people of Israel but it meant the possible redemption of all of humanity throughout all of history, so that as long as we have faith and we believe in Christ, Christ, too, is our atoning sacrifice. And through Christ's resurrection, Christ conquered the sin and the death and the evil that separates each one of us from God; through the grace of God found in Christ, our sinfulness is overcome by Christ's death and resurrection. It is overcome by love itself manifested in Christ! Moreover, through this we may learn to have a foundation of love in love itself: Jesus Christ.

This story that is found in the Bible, from the very first verses in Genesis to the very last verses in Revelation, is the greatest love story, *ever*. It is a story of God loving humanity, then humanity in pride, selfishness, arrogance, and disobedience to God (each of these in sinfulness), separating ourselves from God. But God, in his vast love for us, for humanity, for his created beings, wanted for all of us to be in communion with each other once again. So God created a way, and ultimately that led to the sacrifice and resurrection of his own Son; through God's grace and through Christ, each one of us may be redeemed to God, and humanity and creation may be restored, redeemed, reconciled, and renewed in God. It means that we may once again find love, true love of sacrifice and selflessness which emanates from God, and have a foundation for practicing that joyful, fulfilling love in God; out of the joyful, sacrificing, selfless love that is found in Christ, we too may find fulfillment. But it is not a fulfillment that we keep to ourselves, but it is a fulfillment that we are called to share with others. It is a love that Christ asks of us, now as his friends and no longer as servants, so that we may love one another as Christ has loved us.

Christ asks us to show this practice of love to one another: this includes our neighbors, the people around us, and even our enemies. What does this sacrificing and selfless love look like in your life? How does sacrificing and selfless love transform your relationship with your husband, your wife, your fiance, your boyfriend, your girlfriend, your brother, your sister (and your brothers and sisters in Christ), your father, your mother, your coworkers, your friends, and even your friends who you find to be just a bit annoying? What about the person who cuts you off while you're driving? How does this view of a sacrificing and selfless practice of love, of loving others in the same way that Christ loved us, form your relationships with those who you would consider to be your enemies, the people who have done wrong against you, or the people who you hold, for one reason or another, a grudge against?

Christ selflessly died for us so that we may be restored to God, so that this overarching love story between God and humanity throughout all of history may be complete in you, God, Jesus Christ, and the Holy Spirit. How does the idea of sacrifice, whether it is of our time, our interests, our money or other material goods, affect our relationships with all of those people I have listed?

It is a contrast between selfishness and selflessness. Culture, society, the world: they will always tell you to put yourself first. They will tell you to put yourself above others and get what you want or what you think you need even if it is at the expense, manipulation, exploitation, or unjust treatment of others or entire other groups of people. The world, in discussing love, inevitably returns to selfishness. The gospel, on the other hand, implies selflessness; Jesus Christ tells us to put others before ourselves. (A warning though: this is one of the reasons the gospel is so dangerous; it is not selfish, but selfless and sacrificing. Sacrifice and selflessness are problems for a world that promotes manipulation, exploitation, and injustice – all for a selfish purpose – whether it is on behalf of a person, business or corporation, or a government.) Selflessness is what Christ demonstrated in his life; sacrifice and selflessness are what Christ showed with his death on the cross, dying so that humanity may have an opportunity to be restored to communion with God. In this way we can know what love actually is; love is not selfish, but selfless. And through Christ's act of selflessness, our own selfishness, pridefulness, arrogance, and sinfulness are overcome by the power of Christ's resurrection. Ultimately the practice of love, founded in God and demonstrated through sacrifice and selflessness, does conquer sin and our separation from God.

God's Holy Spirit works in us and creates in us a new and restored person, that we may show what true, holy, sacrificing and selfless love is to our family, friends, and even our enemies. Christ instructs us: "This is my commandment, that you love one another as I have loved you." Demonstrate and practice this fulfilling yet sacrificing and selfless love, in obedience to God, in your lives and in your relationships with all who you encounter.

If you enjoyed these stories, please visit the author's blog, "**The Kayaking Church**," at www.thekayakingchurch.com.

Follow "**The Kayaking Church**" on Twitter!
@kayakingchurch

"An Intertwined Reality: Short Stories for the Already but Not Yet" and the material within this book are the property of the author, Eric Verbovszky. Please do not steal, take, copy, plagiarize, or use (or whatever other terms you would like to use that can be considered synonyms of "steal," "take," "copy," "plagiarize," or "use") any of the author's writing without his express written permission.

However, please feel free to promote this book, and a message of *selfless* love, to all the people that you encounter!

"*Selflessness* is what will conquer the *selfishness* that ravages our world."

Made in United States
Troutdale, OR
02/19/2024

17802742R00086